JOHN ALFRED HEPWORTH was born in Pinjarra, Western Australia, in 1921 and attended Perth Modern School.

He served in the AIF in World War II, travelling to the Middle East, Ceylon and New Guinea. Australia's year-long struggle to take the northern coast of New Guinea informed *The Long Green Shore*, which was commended in a 1949 *Sydney Morning Herald* literary competition and compared to Mailer's *The Naked and the Dead*.

The manuscript was rejected by an English publisher who felt that there were too many war books. Hepworth turned to journalism, poetry and drama, though he occasionally tinkered with his novel.

In the 1960s a number of his plays were performed, and in the following decade he gained prominence through his 'Outsight' column in the *Nation Review*, a magazine he edited for several years. Hepworth then penned columns for the controversial *Toorak Times*.

From the early 1980s onwards he wrote many books, some with Bob Ellis and others illustrated by Michael Leunig.

For two decades Hepworth worked at the ABC, where he was chief subeditor on the Radio Australia news desk. He lived in Melbourne, and had a long relationship with the playwright Oriel Gray—the couple had two sons—and later with his wife Margaret.

John Hepworth died in 1995, soon after learning that *The Long Green Shore* would finally go into print. Ellis, who was instrumental in getting the book published, in an introduction put its closing soliloquy on par with the Gettysburg Address. Critics hailed it as a classic war novel, and for some time a film adaptation was to be Russell Crowe's directorial debut.

LLOYD JONES lives in Wellington. His best-known works include *Mister Pip*, winner of the Commonwealth Writers' Prize and shortlisted for the Man Booker Prize, *The Book of Fame* and *Hand Me Down World*. His acclaimed memoir *A History of Silence* was published in 2013.

ALSO BY JOHN HEPWORTH

Non-fiction
*John Hepworth…His Book* (edited by Morris Lurie, illustrated by Michael Leunig)
*Boozing Out in Melbourne Pubs* (with John Hindle, illustrated by Bloo Souter)
*Around the Bend* (with John Hindle, illustrated by Geoff Prior)
*The Little Australian Library* (illustrated by Keith Brown)
Colonial Capers series

Fiction
*The Multitude of Tigers* (illustrated by Michael Leunig)

For children
*Top Kid* (with Bob Ellis)
*The Paper Boy* (with Bob Ellis)
*The Big Wish* (with Steve J. Spears)
*Looloobelle the Lizard* (illustrated by Frank Hellard)
*Hunting the Not Fair* (illustrated by Nick Donkin)

# The Long Green Shore
## John Hepworth

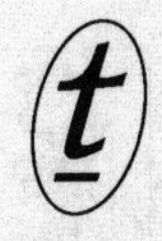

Text Publishing Melbourne Australia

textclassics.com.au
textpublishing.com.au

The Text Publishing Company
Swann House
22 William Street
Melbourne Victoria 3000
Australia



First published by Picador, Pan Macmillan Australia 1995
This edition published by The Text Publishing Company 2014

Cover design by WH Chong
Page design by Text
Typeset by Midland Typesetters

Printed in Australia by Griffin Press, an Accredited ISO AS/NZS 14001:2004 Environmental Management System printer

Primary print ISBN: 9781922147820
Ebook ISBN: 9781922148810
Author: Hepworth, John, 1921– author.
Title: The long green shore / by John Hepworth; introduced by Lloyd Jones.
Series: Text classics.
Subjects: World War, 1939–1945—Campaigns—New Guinea—Fiction.
Other Authors/Contributors: Jones, Lloyd.
Dewey Number: A823.3

This book is printed on paper certified against the Forest Stewardship Council® Standards. Griffin Press holds FSC chain-of-custody certification SGS-COC-005088. FSC promotes environmentally responsible, socially beneficial and economically viable management of the world's forests.

# CONTENTS

# Final Dispatches
## *by Lloyd Jones*

THE paths of two war novelists, John Hepworth and Norman Mailer, crossed in a geographical sense, as well as in literary fortune. Mailer spent a muggy Christmas Day in 1944 aboard an American troopship in Hollandia Bay, in Papua New Guinea. At the same time, Hepworth was ashore, dodging snipers, and wishing for a bath. Both Mailer's *The Naked and the Dead* and Hepworth's *The Long Green Shore* begin in the hold of a troopship. In Hepworth's account, 'There is always a stench, a slave smell.'

Fresh from the war both Mailer and Hepworth are told by publishers that the last thing anyone wishes to read is a book about the war. Mailer persists, shopping his manuscript around until it finds a willing publisher. *The Naked and the Dead* will go on to occupy a spot on the *New York Times* bestseller list for nearly a year, and provide the young writer and his new wife with enough money to sail to Paris and live the expat life at a dollar a day while attending the Sorbonne on the GI Bill.

Hepworth, back in Australia, is less fortunate. It seems he accepted the verdict of the one publisher he sent the manuscript to, Macmillan in London, as the final word on the matter. He shoves his manuscript in the drawer, where, according to Bob Ellis, a friend and colleague of Hepworth, it will remain for many decades, until its eventual publication by Picador in 1995—not long after the author's death.

In Ellis's preface to the first edition we learn that the 28-year-old Hepworth wrote the novel in response to a literary competition run by the *Sydney Morning Herald*. (It was highly commended in 1949.) It is hard to believe that a competition could have provided singular motivation for such an assured debut.

Fifty years on from the 1948 release of *The Naked and the Dead*, writing in the preface to the anniversary edition, Mailer describes his novel as the work of an 'amateur'. He also refers to himself in the third person, as I suppose one might view one's callow youth from the distance of old age. But as Mailer notes, 'the book had vigour. That is the felicity of good books by amateurs.'

Hepworth's novel has none of the same defects; no lacing of nouns with adjectives, 'none of the bestseller style' that Mailer charges his own book with.

I think it is safe to say that neither novel would have been written without the authors' respective war experiences. But by temperament and literary ambition the two works fly in different directions.

The ambition behind *The Long Green Shore* was never

to 'out-write' others or to launch the author into the literary firmament. Hepworth's project is more modest, but no less serious for it. His aim was to transcribe an experience as truthfully as possible. And perhaps it is true to say of soldier-novelists that they have two audiences—those of us content to read from the armchair at home and those they went to war with. The second audience is bound to have a chastening effect on any exuberance or over-egging of the realities of war.

The tone of the young Hepworth's prose is entirely trustworthy. Undoubtedly some serious reading lies behind its understatedness. A hard-earned experience transcends its literary style. Hepworth's task is to speak honestly about the manner of a soldier's death: this often arrives without any warning, although the march along the long green shore might be regarded as one long rehearsal for such a moment; at times it is as though death already occupies a soldier's soul and he is simply waiting on his final dispatch.

Fear sits differently in soldiers. Hepworth seems well acquainted with its varying thresholds and black humour. Whispering John, one of the older characters, sniggers with satisfaction at his good luck to date. 'The young blokes crack up and the old soldier keeps on going, eh?' It is a false boast, as he well knows; his own end is simply forestalled.

Now and then the presiding eye of the narrative takes a step back, such as in the opening scene, declaring that this is no ordinary war novel.

> We sailed that last night through the tail end of a hurricane sea. We came up and ran naked on the open canvas square of the battened hatches,

> standing taut and breathless against the ecstasy of cleanliness in the driving rain...There was a spirit of carnival, a revelry of cleanliness and nakedness in the rain, with the combed wind sweeping the open deck and voices shouting and laughing in the storm while the darkened ship plunged through the rolling seas.

Between moments of barbarity and banality are occasions of great beauty, and for much of the time *The Long Green Shore* is a young soldier's paean to the puzzling thrill of being alive.

The most enduring novels about World War II turned out to be satirical—Joseph Heller's *Catch-22* and, for capturing the vulgarity and absurdity of war, Kurt Vonnegut's *Slaughterhouse 5* is in my view without peer.

The most talked-about war novel in recent times is *Yellow Birds* by Kevin Powers, which draws on his experience as a marine in Iraq. The reader walks in the combatant's boots, and hears the dry rasp of his heart and mind. There is no attempt to draw big lessons. No geopolitical agenda, just one man's experience of being cast like chaff into a horror zone. At times, Powers is guilty of prettifying the experience, which is as problematic as the poet who surrenders genuine grief to poetic form. Perversely, art ends up destroying that which it wished to preserve. In the case of the broken-hearted poet, why write a poem? Why not jump off a bridge?

*The Long Green Shore* is written from a different place. It is an act of remembering mates who died—and, as it happens, did so unnecessarily. The enemy which Command is so eager to engage with is less interested in the Australians. For all that the march mattered, the platoon might as well have found a place on the beach and played volleyball until the end of the war.

Towards the end of the novel, word of the catastrophic nuclear bombing of Hiroshima and Nagasaki filters down to this remote area of fighting in the South Pacific. The deaths of various mates and acquaintances have already been soberly accounted. The news from Japan creates a new frame for what we have learned so far.

It is a breathtaking moment in which the futility of everything the soldiers on the long green march have gone through is painfully clear. It is clear too that this novel has earned its place on the shelves. I hope it endures.

*The Long Green Shore*

# AUTHOR'S NOTE

From the last Christmas of the Second World War, until that war ended, two brigades of the Sixth Australian Infantry Division fought an obscure but at times bitter and bloody campaign along the savage north coast of New Guinea.

When the war ended, and the snakeskin drums sounded the word through the mountains, they were within sight of the deathly valley of the Sepik.

This campaign from Aitape to Wewak was an unnecessary one. The Japanese army in the area was isolated from the rest of the Pacific. They occupied no strategically important ground: they showed no aggressive intent.

This campaign was war in its classic wastefulness. It was fought for no apparent reason, other than that Australia might claim another Division in action; and, perhaps, strengthen her voice with their bodies at the Peace table.

To that end, a few hundred men died.

I know it is not such a great number in the millions of the dead—but it is bitter that they might have died in a better cause.

*The Long Green Shore* is not, strictly, the story of this campaign. But I have chosen it as the framework because here the battle itself has no importance other than individual life and death, and this allows a sharper drawing of men's awareness of life and death. The victory of the Desert, the defeat in Greece, the drowning, gaunt agony of the Kokoda Trail would not have allowed quite the same delineation.

This is essentially a true book, though many of the incidents did not happen in this piece of war, but to other men in other campaigns. The men are true men, but none is one man entire—each is a synthesis of half a dozen or more.

This is the Australian soldier as he is...with something about him essentially national; but, at the same time, basically the same man at war as the legionnaires who crossed the world with Alexander, or the commando who marched with Xenophon through Asia Minor.

It is a long time ago, as our time goes. We who were young begin to grow old.

They have carried the dead out of the green and drifting sea of the rainforest and planted them row by row in domestic earth.

The world is not at peace. But it will be. Surely it will be. One day.

*J. H.*

# 1

We sailed that last night through the tail end of a hurricane sea. We came up and ran naked on the open canvas square of the battened hatches, standing taut and breathless against the ecstasy of cleanliness in the driving rain.

We scooped water from the pools that gathered in the folds of canvas and lathered the fresh foam of soap on our salt-dry bodies. We lined up for the plunge under the showers where the rain guttered off the gun platforms and deck housing in fat shuddering streams.

It was the first freshwater bath we had had for a week. There was a spirit of carnival, a revelry of cleanliness and nakedness in the rain, with the combed wind sweeping the open deck and voices shouting and laughing in the storm while the darkened ship plunged through the rolling seas.

*

Pez and Janos came in naked from the rain bath on the deck, blundering through the double blackout curtains in the roll of the ship, and climbed gingerly down the thin steel stairway into the moist stench of the hold.

There is always a stench, a slave smell, in the hold of a troopship. The stink clings to your clothes and skin long after you climb up into the fresh air.

They picked their way through the crowded well of the hold, dodging the bawdy salutes of their mates to their nakedness, and entered into the maze of bunks massed in double tiers five high.

As they dried themselves on greasy towels in the cramped alleyway between the bunks, Janos wrinkled his nose: 'I can't stand this stink—you could cut it with a spoon.'

Janos was a tall, lean lad from the rich and rugged floodlands of the New South Wales north coast. He had a strong, bony face, a wry mouth and clear grey eyes. His nose was broken and crooked in a way that sundry women had found intriguing.

'Broke her that many times playing football,' he'd tell you, 'decided last time to let her stay broke and I've never had any trouble with her since.'

He came from Grafton where jacaranda blooms and strange tales are told of what happens when the blue flower bursts.

'It's the fever,' he said, 'the jacaranda fever. You can see it in the wenches when they walk the street—the way they swing their hips and carry their breasts proud and look sideways at you with that summer look in their eyes.

You've got to step careful at night in the long grass down by the river. It's a great thing to be young and have your strength and be in Grafton when the jacaranda blooms.

'And there is a legend that any wench whose head you tilt to kiss beneath a jacaranda tree, who does not have the same colour shining in her eyes, then she, poor girl, will die a virgin.' He grins: 'The legend has been proved in part—concerning those whose eyes *do* shine.'

As Janos dragged his jungle green shirt off the bed, the leather wallet fell out and dropped open on the floor. Pez picked it up and handed it back to him, glancing as he did so at the photo framed in the celluloid panel.

'Janice on top tonight,' he observed. 'Is little Mary out of favour?'

'No,' said Janos, 'Janice is on view tonight in memory of things lost but not forgotten. She was a sweet little thing and accommodating too, and it is my great regret that she had a husband.'

Janice had been a part of the jacaranda fever. A buxom lass, she was—a rich northern dish of milk and honey. That night he was in her room at the pub and her husband came home unexpectedly—well, maybe a husband wouldn't appreciate a perfectly reasonable explanation concerning the aphrodisiac effect of the blooming of a blue flower, so Janos went out the window—taking most of his clothes with him, but forgetting his hat. For weeks afterwards a brawny citizen haunted the pubs, tenderly enquiring if any of the AIF boys had lost a hat.

'Hell, that reminds me,' said Pez. 'I should write to Helen tonight—haven't written since we left Cairns.'

'Write tomorrow when we get ashore—she'll get it just as soon.'

'Yeah, tomorrow we're ashore,' said Pez, 'and maybe soon it won't matter whether I wrote or not.'

'Cheerful bastard, aren't you?' grinned Janos. 'I can't stand this stink—I'm going to sleep up on deck, rain or no rain.'

'I'll take a wander round and see what the troops are doing first,' said Pez. 'I'll be with you later.'

All the card players were gathered at the tables or on blankets spread in the open space in the well of the hold. Those who had money still played poker. Those who were broke, watched, or played bridge and five hundred. A few were already half-asleep on their bunks, the sweat streaming from them. Others, where the lights on their beds were good enough, read or wrote. Not many were writing letters—there was nothing much to say—but there was plenty of literature available.

We had received a comforts parcel the day before—you remember those parcels that a benevolent nation distributed for your cultural relaxation and entertainment on shipboard. There were a great number of inspired novelettes in gaudy paper covers with such titles as *The Corpse on Fifth Avenue* and *The Corpse with the Missing Face* and *Gunfire at Rustlers Gulch*. And they tried to tell us there was a paper shortage back home.

But these well-wishers thought of the physical as well as the spiritual man. There was also in each parcel a tin of very sticky lollies, a handkerchief, a pair of socks, a tube of toothpaste which was admirable for cleaning rifle barrels and polishing metal souvenirs, and, of course, a cake of soap.

A grateful country looks after its men when they are going into battle. 'Nothing,' as Dick the Barber remarked sourly when we opened the parcels, 'is too good for the Australian soldier.'

Pez made his way down the alleys between the bunks.

There was Regan lying on his bunk—the top one of the tier, with the luxury of direct lighting and an overhead air vent that roared gently in amplification of the sound that you heard when you were a kid and pressed a shell against your ear to hear the roar of the sea.

Regan lay in his bunk in fractional comfort, his body sticky and sweating and his face and throat bathed in the thick, cool jet of air. He was a thin lad in his twenties with a ragged thatch of black hair, a thin, swarthy, Irish face and close-set blue eyes.

He was holding a paper-backed novel, but he wasn't reading. He was lying there, staring at the blurred page and feeling fear in his heart. It had always been the same for him—this fear of being hurt and the greater fear of people knowing that he was afraid.

Pez passed on and paused to watch the poker game for a moment. He saw Cairo Fleming grin and bluff his last pound on a pair of deuces. And when old Whispering John called him on an ace-high blue, he laughed. He got up from the table broke, and he grinned: 'Hell, Mrs Kelly wouldn't let her little boy Ned play with you blokes.'

You can tell a lot from the way a man plays poker—especially the way he loses.

Old Whispering John always played his cards with elaborate cunning, close to the vest. Next hand he was first to bet.

'I'll make it a modest sixteen shillings,' he whispered.

Brogan's hand went into the pack and young Griffo made it twenty-four. Sunny and Ocker both threw in and it was up to John again.

'You can't make it twenty-four,' said Whispering John querulously. 'It was only a four-bob game.'

'I made it eight for cards,' said Griffo. 'You made it sixteen yourself, first bet.'

Whispering John looked hard at young Griffo and felt hatred for this youth who sat looking at him with elaborate unconcern and a womanish mouth.

'I wish to Christ I knew what you had in your hand,' John whined.

'There's one sure way to find out,' said Sunny.

'All right, all right!' snapped Whispering John. Anyone'd think I didn't have the guts to look.' He held his cards up between a bony thumb and forefinger. He was breathing unevenly.

Young Griffo laid down three queens.

'Six tits,' he said.

Whispering John slammed his cards down with petty viciousness on the table: 'I had three tens,' he complained. 'I get three tens and he has three queens. He's been got at, the bastard. He's been touched. Christ, I never seen such paper as I'm getting tonight.' He pushed the stool back and stood up, 'That finishes me—when your luck runs that way it's time to get out.'

Pez threaded his way back into the alleys between the bunks.

There was a group around the Laird, who swung gently in the hammock he had scrounged from the crew's quarters and slung between two iron stanchions so that it was in the cool spot right under the big ventilator shaft.

'Well, I don't know,' boomed the Laird, 'but I'll make a bet that fifty per cent of these skulls we've got get themselves killed or go troppo within a week.' He snarled with fine scorn: 'Duntroon boys! My God, what hoons! What drongos! After seeing their form it's my considered opinion that they couldn't lead their old grandmothers to the company latrine.

'You know that little bloke?' he said. 'You know, that smooth-faced snotty little bloke with the curly hair—what do they call him?—Billy the Kid, that's right...' His voice dropped to a horrified rumble: 'Do you know what he tried to make me do at Redlynch, just before we got on the boat? He tried to make me do rifle exercises by numbers! I've been in the army four years and that hairy-arsed schoolboy comes along and wants me to do rifle exercises by numbers. I told him what he could do with the rifle—by number, too, and bayonet end first.'

Said Dick the Barber: 'Well, I don't know, you can't always tell by the way a bloke looks—remember Bosker?'

'Who's he?' asked Bishie. 'Not that big major up at Brigade?'

'No,' said Dick the Barber. 'He was a lairy little bloke, Bosker, with a kind of Haw Haw voice and an absolute nut about having your buttons done up. He got killed at Sananada—but he did a bloody good job.'

'Yeah,' said the Laird. 'He should have got a VC for that job—he earned it.'

Pez remembered that day. Three times Bosker had gone through that desolate waste of swamp and palms, where the shells were falling, to carry orders to 'A' Company, pinned down on the flank. The fourth time he died in the swamp.

'But I wouldn't worry too much about these apes of officers we've got,' Dick the Barber was saying. 'When you get down to it, who does the work? The poor old drack private and the corporal. The corporal—he's the leader—he's the one that actually takes the men in and does the job after all the brass hats have finished deciding what the job is. And we've got better corporals than any other army in the world.'

Said Bishie: 'If it comes to that, we can always shoot the skulls first and carry on from there.'

But Dick the Barber was talking: 'And you know there's men on this boat that aren't even getting their efficiency pay. Brass hats—brass bastards! They're going to send those men in and ask them to go forward scout and they won't even give them efficiency pay.

'Christ, it's an insult! They say to a man: "Now, if you're a good boy for six months, and you don't go ack-willie, and you know how to fire a Bren gun, and you can do your bloody gas drill that you'll never bloody need—then we'll open our great big brass hearts and give you an extra zac a day."

'Sixpence a day! A lousy zac! Christ, you'd think they were giving you gilt-edged security for life! Some of these blokes over-stayed their leave a couple of days—or else they shot into town and got drunk—so they took the lousy zac a day off them.'

His voice jumbled with bitterness and anger: 'So they reckon they're not efficient soldiers, but they're still going to send them into action. They ought to be cut up and their swags burnt!'

'Now, now, Dick,' grinned Bishie, 'don't get yourself excited.'

'Why the hell shouldn't I get excited?' snapped Dick the Barber. 'That's the trouble with the world—people don't get excited about these things.'

'Sure,' cut in Harry Drew quietly. 'But it's a waste of time and energy, getting excited and not doing anything. We'll fix a deputation to Slapsy Paint tomorrow and see if we can get anything done about it.'

The Laird heaved his bulk up in the hammock and leaned on one elbow as he chuckled reminiscently: 'You know, I had a mate once like that. If anything went wrong he'd scream and tear his hair and stamp around cursing and swearing better than any bullocky.

'He was with me when I was up the scrub—a little bloke, sandy hair, name of Samuels—and a bloody good mate, too. You might know his brother, Dick—he had a brother, Alec, I think his name was. He was a dentist down the 'Gong.'

Dick the Barber reflected. 'A thin dark-haired bloke with a bit of a twisty eye?'

'No,' said the Laird, 'he was a big fair-haired snodger—hell of a nice bloke but always getting into strife with married women.'

'I can't place him,' said Dick the Barber ruminatingly. 'Can't place him anywhere round the 'Gong.'

'Oh, well,' admitted the Laird, 'I wouldn't be certain it was down the south coast—might have been out Wagga way he lived.'

'Think I'll hit the cot,' said Harry Drew, rising and stretching. 'We'll be in tomorrow, I guess.'

'Yeah, we'll see her tomorrow.'

Bishie stared sombrely ahead. He was new to this mob, he'd come out of the militia. He was remembering the last time—a different time to the one they knew and he could not really share it with them.

He remembered the smell of smoke and blood. Behind them Rabaul was burning and they fled through the jungle and the swamp with the dry mouths of fear.

This time they wouldn't have to run.

Cairo Fleming stood hunched over the rail in the deeper shadow of a lifeboat and stared down at the boiling blue sparks of phosphorescence in the white foam furrowed from the ship's bow. He knew the feel of the sea—the wild, swift bucking of a small and slippery deck and the sting of the combed salt spray as the fishing smack butted jauntily into the long, grey rollers of the South Pacific. Toes, naked, gripping the smooth surging deck...The small comforting smell of oil and engines in the gulf of wind and sea...The nets running out, dropping out behind in the grey water...The squirming, heavy weight of them when they were hauled in and the slower, heavy bite of the boat in the running seas to home...

Cairo stared at the blue and boiling sparks and felt the surge of the deck as a memory. Inside the heavy army boots, his lean toes instinctively crooked and clung, as though his trousers were again rolled to his knees and his feet planted, balanced apart, gripping the small deck. And in the foam and the darkness of the sea and the hurricane-grey sky and the timeless surge, he felt his loneliness—that loneliness and nostalgic discontent he knew all his life.

He knew what they used to say: 'Cairo's always happy,' they used to say. 'You never see Cairo without a grin on his face.'

The Laird used to tell about him and Cairo in the Owen Stanley show: coming up the track from Popandetta, the Nips opened up with a mountain gun. Cairo dives for a hole and then props when he sees a considerably dead Nip sitting up in her. Then one lands a bit close and the shrap whistles through the trees. Cairo says to the dead Nip: 'Brother, I need that hole more than you,' and he leans down, grabs him by the collar, hauls most of him out and dives in just as another one bursts about five yards away.

No one ever knew whether Cairo was blown or jumped into that hole—Cairo himself thinks he maybe got some assistance.

And again at Sananada, the Laird would tell: We were cut off for a bit and things looked sticky. Cairo says nothing to us, but goes quietly to Coulter—Captain Coulter, his third pip came through not long before and he had charge of the Company then—he got killed a couple of days later, remember—Cairo says to Coulter: 'Look, I don't mind seeing if I can get back to the battalion—we might get some help.'

And Coulter turned on him: 'Get back to your bloody section, Fleming,' he said. 'You're too good a bloody soldier to lose trying this VC stuff.'

Cairo shrugs, and says OK, and starts back. But he'd only gone a few steps when Coulter calls him: 'Thanks mate,' he says.

Poor old Coulter copped it two days later—shrapnel in the guts. He was a good man. He died hard.

Sure, he always had a grin, had Cairo. He was always happy—though sometimes when he grinned he wasn't happy.

It's bad, the loneliness of being apart from humanity when you want desperately to be part. It keeps you awake like a hunger in the night. And even when people do accept you, there is always that doubt, that fear in the mind that they may be doing it consciously out of pity, or condescendingly to flatter their own egos. It is a burning thing, that fear—it scorches the clean flesh of your pride.

'Hell,' thought Cairo. 'I'm being sorry for myself.'

He grinned wryly in the darkness and the twisting of his broad mouth showed strong white teeth. It was a strong face—a round, heavy jaw and broad mouth and nostrils, deep brow, soft brown eyes and crinkly black hair. His body was lean and hard and his hands slender, the fingers thin and strong.

'Hell,' he thought. 'What does it matter? Tomorrow we land and after that...'

A vague figure blundered a little, missing the roll of the boat, collided with the frame of a lifeboat derrick and cursed casually.

'That you, Log?' said Cairo.

'Yeah,' said the Log. 'Where are you?'

'Over here near the rail—watch the rope.'

Log groped his way to the rail, rested his elbows on it and hunched down beside Cairo.

'What are you doing, mate?' he asked.

'Just thinking,' said Cairo.

'Problems?'

'No—just thinking.'

They slouched there watching a drunken star that staggered on the northern horizon. They were comfortably silent for a long time. Cairo felt a strange contentment in the surging of the ship...

Deacon had been lying on his bunk, his eyes closed, the sticky trickle of sweat on his body, trying to sleep.

But instead of sleep he drifted back always into the dream—until in the end he was forcing himself to stay in the half-darkness of the mind and striving to re-create the look of her and the sound of her voice and the scenes they had moved through together.

The heat and stench and sweat of the hold, the throbbing of the ship and babble of voices from the Laird and Bishie and Dick the Barber talking down the alley, he forced away until they were resting thinly on the skin of his brain and he was burrowed deep into the warm darkness of his memory.

He felt a faint, pleasant stirring of the bowels as he conjured. They were lying in the long, sun-warm grass on the banks of the river. The wattles grew low over them and made a cool, thin cavern of shade. The golden pollen drifted down as a small breeze rustled the branches. Some of it had powdered the deep auburn of her hair and he noticed it as she turned to him.

Her cropped auburn hair, with the small curls clinging round her head like that sculpture of the Greek boy in the museum. Her eyes shining, her tip-tilted nose powdered with freckles and her rich mouth slightly open and wry with desire.

His arm was around her shoulders and she turned her soft, firm young body urgently to his. The feeling of the sun warming and the earth and green things growing and the sap singing...

His mind hinged on this sequence and he couldn't force the imagery on past that point. The memory of her turning to him blurred into the sun and the earth and the trees.

Three times he forced the image up and each time it blurred. With a small curse of frustration, he sat up suddenly. He reached under the pack and the illegal lifebelt which made up his pillow, and took out a leather wallet. He opened it and drew a folded letter from among the small pack of photographs in the celluloid-covered compartment. The letter was grimy on the edges from handling. Deacon leaned on one elbow, part way out of his bunk to catch the light, and read it again.

That young, flourishing, artificial script...

*Oh My Darling,*

*I cried all night after you had gone and next morning the girls at the office were very sticky about why my eyes were so red. But I wouldn't tell them. I couldn't tell anyone about us and how I feel for you.*

*Everything has been black and miserable since you left me and the only thing that lets me go on living (the only thing that <u>makes</u> me want to go on living) is the thought that this time will be the last time that you will be away.*

*I am jealous of all the other times you went away and it was not <u>me</u> that felt sick in the heart when you were gone. (Do you really think I am jealous of you, darling? I am! I'm terribly jealous! Do you think that is a bad thing?) I hate all those other women you have known. You are the first man I have ever truly loved and I wish I could be the first one for you, like you are for me.*

*I know you will laugh at me, but perhaps men never feel the same way about these things as a woman. And I <u>am</u> a woman now, my darling—you made me that, even if you haven't made me an honest one yet. But you will, won't you? You do want to marry me, don't you?*

*It's different for a man, I know, but sometimes I get terrible black depressions and I am sure that you never truly loved me and I am so desolate and miserable and I could kill myself. Other times I just wake up in the morning and I am sure, for no good reason, that you do love me and you will come back.*

*Oh, I'm a shameless woman, I know I am, my darling. I gave you my body and I suppose I really am a very immoral person and I ought to feel ashamed when I sit opposite Mummy at breakfast.*

*But I don't, my darling, I don't! I feel very proud and very happy—that is, when I'm not feeling very small and very miserable and certain that you don't love me.*

*Oh, come home soon, darling. Look after yourself and come home soon so that I can be an abandoned woman and be yours again.*

*Goodbye for a while, a little while, my darling.*

*Margaret*

Deacon finished reading, but stayed, leaning on one elbow, staring at, but not seeing, the written page. He could feel a pride of conquest and an egotistical glow at the extravagance of her abandonment. She was so young and theatrical, with such a young passion for being in love with love.

You told lies to a woman and tried to weave those lies into a pattern to make the whole affair a golden tapestry, a piece of artistry, a highly skilled game. You never found in your beloved Margaret that depth and sincerity of emotion you thought to find in love when you were young.

When you were young, Deacon! The romantic bitterness and weight of twenty-two years made you mourn for the time 'when you were young'.

This beloved Margaret had touched but never torn your heart. Everything you did or said had a cold shadow of calculation in it. 'It's got to stop,' Deacon thought.

The labour of weaving patterns in words and keeping up the pretence was too great, the game was palling. But there must be some way to let her down easy—to break it up but leave her with the shine in her eyes and the warm, eager parting of her lips.

Oh, when we are arrogant enough to believe that we have created love in a woman, Deacon, we must condescend to handle her very gently. Even when we break her heart we must make sure that we find some pattern that relieves us of the burden, but provides that she still must love us. 'There must be some way that wouldn't hurt her,' was the way Deacon thought of it.

'Hey! What are you perving on?' said Fluffy, pausing by the bunk. 'Where'd you get the letter? Carrier pigeon service?'

'No,' said Deacon, folding it quickly but casually. 'It's an old one.'

'One from the steady, eh?' said Fluffy, grinning. 'It'll do you no good reading that sort of thing now, boy. It'll give you bad dreams. You'll be sleeping next to nothing warm or soft for the next year or so. Better forget her. Hank the Yank's probably in, anyway.' He grinned, and passed on down the alley.

Fluffy. A tough kid from Waterloo. A tough kid who talked tough, but mostly because he had seen too many films. He was a good lad. He was to die on the bank of a muddy river with machine-gun bullets stitched across his guts.

'Tomorrow,' thought Deacon, 'we'll land. We'll be able to post mail.' He dragged out his writing pad and scrawled his number, rank, name and unit across the top of the page. Then...'Beloved Margaret,' he wrote, with a little flourish.

He paused, chewing the top of his pencil. Down the alley he could hear Dick the Barber holding forth: 'Well, I wonder how Killer Connell's feeling tonight. He's been sweating for action ever since he came to us, and now it looks like he'll get it.'

Lieutenant-Colonel Connell, using only his right hand, levered the stopper out of the whisky bottle with his thumb and poured a stiff nobbler into his own and the Doctor's glasses. Killer Connell they called him, but the title did not derive from his exploits on the field.

It was that day on the Tablelands when we were practising for the Divisional parade. The battalion ground was a naked brown field shimmering in the burning sun.

As the platoons and companies broke off from the square and marched in a long battalion column round the field and past the saluting base, Connell stood under the shade of the trees, screaming: 'Swing your arms! Lengthen your step! Come on, "A" Company! Come on, Pioneers! Call yourselves soldiers—Jesus Christ, a mob of Palmer Street whores could march better than that!'

And the word was muttered round from mouth to mouth as they marched: 'The old boy didn't get home till five o'clock this morning—down on the nest with that nurse of his at Atherton.'

'Maybe she knocked him back,' someone suggested. 'Maybe that's what's wrong with him—he didn't get a bit last night.'

Two strays, shaggy friendly mongrels that had been straying round the camp for days, came running and yelping onto the parade ground in front of the column.

'Battalion, halt!' screamed Connell.

As the troops bunched up to the halt they could see him making his way across to the back of the parade ground and hear him yelling for the RPs.

'Sergeant Hino! Sergeant Hino!' he yelled. 'Where the bloody hell are you when you're bloody well called?'

'A nice way he talks to men,' muttered Janos satirically.

Hino, the fat little Regimental Provost, was coming at an agitated trot from where he had been stationed at the far corner of the field. Connell made towards him with long, angry strides. We couldn't hear what was being said but we could see Connell gesturing angrily and Hino standing there trembling and stammering, 'Yes, Sir! No, Sir!' and nearly knocking out what little brains he had, he saluted so hard when Connell dismissed him.

The troops stood relaxed, resting their rifle butts in the red dust, while Hino and a couple of other RPs tried to catch the frisky, yelping excited dogs.

There were surreptitious grins and muttered comments and a burst of laughter as the little ginger dog eluded the fat and despairing Sergeant Hino by diving between his legs. Then some officer, with an eye on Connell, would snap over his shoulder in his best Duntroon voice: 'Quiet, "A" Company! Stop that laughing!'

But Connell had walked back under the shade and was standing with his back to the parade. His hands clasped behind him, he stared with pale and unblinking eyes into the grey-green thickets of timber that stretched away to the left of the camp. His mouth was tight, his shoulders hunched, the fingers of his clasped right hand twitched and his breathing was ragged.

The RPs eventually caught the dogs and led them off. The Adjutant gave the order and the long column swung again into the march past. All the Company officers were rallying their men.

'Come on! Come on now, Fourteen Platoon!'

'Hansen, pick up that step!'

'Knight, straighten that rifle!'

'Johnson, swing that arm higher! Higher! Higher! Right up to the shoulders!'

Running up and down the flanks of their platoons: 'Lef, ri! Lef, ri!' Harrying them like sheepdogs—yapping like sheepdogs. But Connell still stood with his back to the parade, his hands clasped behind him, staring out through the trees.

They were halfway round for the second time when they heard the shots—two spaced reports echoing thinly from down the scrub—and heads twitched at the sound. 'What was it?' 'Not a rifle...' 'Revolver, I think.'

Connell turned back to the parade and started screaming again. Now there was a sort of satisfaction in his voice: 'Come on, march!' he bellowed. 'I'll stay here all day if necessary. I'll march you round and round and round this bloody square until you drop or do it right!'

Word filtered back through the grapevine of the marching men. 'It was the dogs. He had the dogs shot, the bastard!'

They marched stubbornly. You could feel their bitter silence through the thud of their heavy boots and the beating of the brass band. Round and round they went. Then Connell stopped them and abused them, and harangued and threatened them. Then they marched again—and again, and again. They marched. They swung their arms and moved their feet, but with a stubborn mediocrity. It could not be attacked as a deliberate and insolent slovenliness, but it was still quite obvious.

The strange duel went on. A clash between a sullen and savage man with the immense mumbo power of discipline and rank behind him, and the vast, silent, stubborn and tangible anger of a thousand men who would have forgiven him many worse things, but could not forgive him shooting two dogs.

And in the end, Connell was beaten and dismissed them. When they broke from their parades there was a strange feeling of triumph and elation through the camp. The lines were filled with voices louder than usual and wild carolling ho-ho-hos and laughter rang through the trees. And the voices and the laughter fell on Connell like a black rain and burned him like acid.

So they called him Killer Connell.

Young Rocky Bennet was foolish enough to write the story of the shooting of the dogs in a letter home. The officer censoring the mail—old Suck'n See Seaton—took it to Connell, who gave Rocky twenty-eight days field punishment.

Lieutenant-Colonel Connell splashed a small quantity of soda into the glass and tossed off the whisky. He and

Doc Maguire were sitting at the small table in Connell's cabin—the whisky bottle was three-parts empty.

'They hate me, Doc,' said Connell. 'That's the way I want them to feel.'

He stared for a moment at the empty glass as he put it down on the table. There was a hard, thin, sensual line round his mouth and nostrils. His pale, harsh blue eyes were a trifle bloodshot and puffiness under the eyes and the nervous skin over the strong Gothic bone of his face showed dissipation and sleeplessness and nerves rubbed raw.

'Men who are happy and contented and well fed don't fight well, Doc,' he said. 'I want 'em lean and hungry and hating me and themselves and everyone else in the world. Then they'll fight! And these boys of mine are going to fight, by Jesus!'

He poured himself another drink and the Doc, who tossed his tot off at one gulp when Connell reached for the bottle, pushed his own glass over for a refill. The Doc never talked much when he was drinking.

'You know, Doc,' said Connell, 'I was bloody near a breakdown on the Tablelands. A man's a fool the way he gets hold of some slut and wears himself out on her...' He sneered at the memory. 'Christ! It doesn't make you feel good. It doesn't make you feel happy or forget. Whoring and drinking. What's the reason, Doc? Why does a man do it?'

'I don't know, Cliff,' said the Doc. 'I'm no psychologist.'

Connell looked at him and his mouth twisted: 'No, you're no psychologist. You're not even much of a doctor—a whisky soak—a drunken quack—the pox doctor's clerk.'

Doc Maguire looked at him steadily, a little blankly. The spirit was starting to work now and he felt the calmly sullen detachment of his drunkenness. He never got falling-down drunk, the Doc—his voice just got a bit slower and more considered and he would stare steadily. The tiny scarlet threads of veins in his cheeks grew brighter, and nothing mattered, nothing touched him.

'How do you reckon you'll go in action the first time, Doc?' sneered Connell. 'It'll be a bit harder than you're used to—harder than sitting in the mess all night soaking whisky and then getting up next morning to dish out a few cascara tablets and aspirin.'

Maguire contemplated Connell and licked his lips slowly. 'You watch your own guts, Cliff,' he said casually. 'I'll watch mine. I'll be all right. I'll be there when I'm wanted. You smash 'em up—I'll patch 'em up.'

Connell's face flushed and hardened: 'You'll address me by my rank, Captain Maguire,' he snapped. 'And remember that I'm your superior officer now.'

Maguire lumbered slowly to his feet, gathered himself half to attention and gave a casual imitation of a salute—looking all the time at Connell with an expression of blank derision. 'Goodnight, Lieutenant-Colonel Connell, DSO and Bar,' he said, and turned towards the door.

As he lifted the latch, Connell spoke. 'Come here, Mag,' he said gruffly.

With his hand still on the latch, Maguire turned slowly: 'Yes, Lieutenant-Colonel?'

'Come here, Mag, for Christ sake. Come and have a drink.'

Connell poured two healthy slugs into the glasses, concentrating his gaze on the measure as he did so. Maguire stayed still for a long moment, staring at Connell's bent head. Then he shrugged his shoulders slightly, let the latch drop and walked back to the table.

The mob round Harry Drew was urging him on, laughing and whooping: 'Rip it up her, boy! Bore it into her! Let her go!'

'All right, all right!' said Harry Drew. 'You think I talk for the sake of talking. But these flabby, time-serving politicians are getting up back home and telling us what we're thinking. Read the papers! The AIF thinks so-and-so. The AIF wants such-and-such. How the hell do they know what we want or think? They never ask us. According to these fat-arse opportunists we just love this war—we can't get enough of it! You know these boys will fight to hell and back, if necessary, and everyone does want to get in and get it over with. But what they really want—the old blokes anyway that have seen it before—is to get back home and stay. No one with any sense breaks his neck to get into a blue. No one really likes killing.'

Harry Drew smoked a stinking pipe and loved an argument. He knew the names of all the Cabinet Ministers and remembered who had sent scrap iron to Japan.

Hell, he was arguing about politics that night we stood on the start line at Tobruk. Full as a boot on army rum, he was, and laying down the law like he had a stand on the

Domain. And he was still arguing—and willing to fight about it—when we moved into the attack.

The card game was breaking up and they were on a couple of rounds of show to finish—one draw and show for two bob a hand to finish the game.

'We'll have another round, eh?' invited Whispering John. He had insinuated himself back into the game—he never stayed out for long—and since he was winning a few shillings he played quickly, with suppressed eagerness and a small, cunning grin on his lips.

'I'll be in another round if you like,' said young Griffo. 'Another dozen if you like—I'm easy.'

'One more round will do me,' said Brogan. 'I'm two quid behind now and I can't see myself picking it up at this game.'

Sunny and Ocker grunted assent and old John flipped the cards round rapidly as they pushed their two bobs to the centre of the table.

'Come on,' he snickered confidentially. 'Put your money in the centre and play like scholars and gentlemen.' He was pleased with his catch-cry. 'This is where you make the money—you come here in motor cars and go home with the arse out of your pants,' he snickered.

'Come on, John,' said Brogan. 'Turn me over two broads—and not too many aces. Finish her quick—we land tomorrow and I want to get some sleep tonight.'

'Yes,' said John as he flipped the cards over, 'you need to sleep tonight—sleep as much as you can—you'll lose a lot from here on.'

*

Regan stirred uneasily in the thick, smothering sleep of the hold. The massed tiers of bunks around him were filled now and thick with heavy breathing and occasional snores. Curly Thomas, in the next bunk, had come up after Regan was asleep and turned the nozzle of the air vent over onto his bunk.

So Curly slept in the comparative comfort of the cool stream of air sucked down from the deck, while Regan sweated and tossed with bad dreams.

Bishie was threading his way through the sleeping tangle of the hold to fill his water bottle at the one tap, located over near the latrines.

The Laird was lying back, half asleep, his hands clasped behind his head, half listening to Dick the Barber.

'You know,' Dick was saying, 'a funny thing happened to a mate of mine once—a little bloke by the name of Spade Burns—you might know him if you worked out west any time.'

Deacon was falling—a slow, sickening fall into darkness—and there was a sudden shock as he threw himself back from the edge of the pit and jerked awake.

He was slouched over on his side and the pencil had fallen from his slackened fingers onto the pad. He looked at the sheet—his number, rank and name were on the top of the page, then: 'Beloved Margaret'. The rest of the page was a blank.

'Ah, hell,' he yawned. 'I'll finish her tomorrow when we get in.'

He put the pad and pencil under his lifebelt pillow and turned over heavily and uncomfortably to sleep. He could hear Dick the Barber's voice down the alley, and a grunted comment from the Laird.

Cairo Fleming put his toothbrush and paste back in the toilet holdall and slipped it back into his haversack. He kicked off his unlaced boots and climbed into the bunk.

'Night, Cairo,' said the Log drowsily from the next bunk.

Cairo closed his eyes. 'Night, mate,' he said.

Lieutenant-Colonel Connell poured the last of the whisky.

'Sluts,' he said. 'They're all sluts and she was as bad as any of them. I was glad to get away from her...'

Doc Maguire looked steadily at him with that same blank derision and made no comment.

Pez and Janos were bedded down in the shelter of a tarpaulin under the forward gun platform in the ship's smell of pitch and hemp. The sharp edge of the wind flicked at them and when the ship rolled it buffeted their shelter, whip-cracking the loose ends of the tarpaulin.

But they were wrapped in a warm cocoon of blankets—their own and some they had borrowed from the sweating sleepers in the hold—and had draped their ground sheets so the water would drain off down through the ropes and not collect underneath them.

They lay silent, rocked in the vast plunge of the ship, and heard the wind howling through the rigging. There is no sound like it on earth—the wind howling on the vast bowstrings of the mast and stays.

'We're riding out of the rain,' said Pez.

You could see the sky ahead was broken and a stormy moon was tossing in a streaming sky.

'Port tomorrow,' said Pez.

'Yeah,' said Janos: 'If the old tub holds together that long.'

Captain Dyall Jones, Master of the *City of Benong*, patted the worn rail of the bridge as a rider pats the foaming neck of his horse after a hard run.

They were a pair, he thought, the ship and he. But for the brutal grace of war, both of them lay in Wreckers' Row.

Chicken farms in Surrey are a dream of the open sea, but when the fowls scratch under your window you dream of the sea again. Chicken farms and a war a-blowing?

He remembered getting out the good black suit and brushing it down—the smell of solid serge and mothballs. The trip to London—the polite disinterest of the Admiralty and the suggestion that this might be a younger man's war. The days and weeks spent sitting on hard wooden benches outside snugly closed office doors. A quiet, solid, stubbornly persistent figure in brushed black, twisting the hard-brimmed hat in his stubborn, ship-wise fingers.

Finally they got tired of his persistence and, in despair, had given him the *City of Benong*—which itself was too old for a young ship's war.

They had been somewhere off the bloody beach of Dunkirk; the stukas had missed them when they ran for Alexandria after Greece fell; and the Son of Heaven had lost them in the darkness out of Malaya.

Captain Dyall Jones eyed the broken sky ahead.

'Keep her steady on that pattern, Mr Johnson. She'll do.'

'Aye, sir,' said Mr Johnson; and thought privately, with immense pride, what monstrous maritime things a man would take to sea in times of war.

Captain Dyall Jones left the bridge and the *City of Benong* sailed out under a sky of streaming cloud and moon.

Pez lay trying to think of home.

He thought: 'I should be calling up pictures of how the fire would be burning in the front room at home on a night like this. And how it would be—coming in out of the rain to the warmth of the fire.'

But the images were all manufactured in words first and then forced into the brain. There was no real picture—no emotional memory.

Even in the thought of Helen there was no warmth—though God knows there had been enough fire between them when they lay together; and a deep, friendly warmth of peace and home on those calm evenings when they sat opposite each other, quietly reading or talking.

And then, of course, there was their problem—three people loving where only two could love. No good thinking about that—there could be no solution yet.

'When the war is over,' she had said. 'When you both come home.' There was loyalty in her—even if loyalty is not always sense. 'I can't write to Bob and tell him it's ended,' she said. 'And when he comes home and I know he's got to go again—I can't tell him then.' She had stared into the fire, her hands clasped against her temples, ruffling the shining brown of her hair. 'And I don't know whether it *has* finished. I know how I feel about you, but I know he needs me. War and loneliness can twist things—you can't just grab what you think you want without thinking if other people have rights.'

The whole business seemed far away now. All you could do was say: 'Sometime—sometime I will again consider hotly the problems of life and love.'

But a man might never measure out that time, or know if it was coming to him.

Maybe that was the solution. If Bob was killed...

You couldn't wish him dead, but it would solve it. There would be no barriers then—no divided loyalties—no question except that answered by the hasty heart.

But there was no reality in that either. That was in the future, and a soldier has no future.

Suddenly he felt the great loneliness of himself upon the earth: the monstrous, lonely howling of the wind was in the rigging; he had lost his past—the future was uncertain; he was alone on a stormy-mooned ocean.

Pez settled back into the rough warmth of his blanket cocoon. He breathed the cold, clean air.

So there was no future—what the hell.

He slept.

# 2

Pez awoke in the first grey dawn, stretched his cramped body on the nest of ropes, crawled out of his blankets and went to the rail.

The *City of Benong* was anchored in the lee of a small island that lay in the mouth of a broad, shallow bay. There was a great mass of shipping gathered in the calm waters of the bay—a war armada of rusty, sea-grey vessels. Invasion barges surged through the tangle. On the distant smooth black sands, a long line of barges were humped half on the beach, half in the water—their jaws flopping open on the sand like clumsy mechanical saurians.

At first glance the green bank of palms and jungle growth seemed solid. But as Pez gazed he saw the long palm-leaf buildings take shape under the camouflage of trees, the distant toy movements of men and trucks, the thin, hazel pennants of smoke from the cook-fires in the camps.

You could pick out ant swarms of activity where they were loading cases on trucks at the food dumps and the flow of movement in the marshalling yards on the beach where they were loading men and equipment into the barges.

Inland, the hazy, fanged, green mountains piled up into the mist of distance. Thick white cloud lay in the valleys and trailing scarves of it clung on the climbing jungle trees of the mountainside.

Pez turned to find where the sunglow was growing—got his bearings and turned to gaze down the long green shore.

This was the way they were going—down there where the trees and the foam and the beach faded into the perspective of sea and sky.

Down past there was Nip country...

Janos joined Pez at the rail.

He yawned: 'Christians awake and greet the happy morn!'

The order is to disembark at ten o'clock sharp. So at eight everyone has been herded up out of the hold and crushed into company lots on the deck with all their gear.

At twelve, we are still there in the open sun on the burning steel deck. At half past, word comes round: there will be no meal—we'll get that ashore—but there is a cup of tea down the galley for those who want it. There is a general scramble for chipped enamel mugs.

The troops are used to this old army habit: run like hell to the start point and then sit on your backside for two hours—move two paces and sit some more.

They are sprawled over the deck, some squatting on their packs playing cards, some reading paper-backed novels, a couple scrawling letters home.

Old Whispering John is still in the poker school. He is still winning and grins delightedly as he shuffles the greasy pack.

Some are slouched over the rails, checking up on landmarks and trying to establish the position of our troops and the Nips: 'Down there, just past that far headland—that's where the Fourth Battalion's holding them.'

Rumour and information—positive if not factual—comes scrambling aboard a troopship along the anchor chain as it drops into the shallows of a new harbour.

The young reinforcements are cocky and elated. They confidently pass on to each other the news that the Nip is starving and disorganised and half-armed. They make profound military assessments. They see this is going to be a snack, with all the glory and no danger. Some of them are condescending and almost sorry for the enemy. They begin to doubt, in their self-mesmerism, whether it is really worthwhile taking the trouble to defeat such a sorry foe. If they go on like this, they will be feeling offended that the brass hats have offered them such a menial glory.

But the old hands are not so complacent. Mud is mud and here they make mountains of it. And a starving animal or a starving man is fierce.

We hear that up the river the Fourth Battalion has struck some opposition from our 'unarmed' foe: three killed yesterday, a couple wounded.

It is the Yankee armada in the bay. They are leaving, sailing north, tomorrow.

We hear for the first time the legend of the nurses—the legend that goes with us down the long green shore. But it is always on a different track—over the other hill.

The Fourth Battalion brought out some Yankee nurses that the Nips had captured in the Philippines, we hear. The Nip officers brought them over with them and have been using them. One of these nurses is in a bad way—rotten with the pox. She begs them not to bring her back. She wants to shoot herself. She smashes a bottle and tries to cut the veins in her wrists. They're down at the hospital now, we are told. You can see it—that long native hut and those tents back behind that wooden tower—you can see the red cross through the trees.

God knows where this legend comes from, but every week or so it revives. Sometimes there are four nurses, sometimes seven. Sometimes the Fourth rescues them, sometimes the Fifth or First. But otherwise the story has the same theme each time—and lots of our blokes believe it and repeat it seriously each time they hear it.

These rumours and legends of the track and camp are the soldiers' literature and radio and vaudeville show. Rumours of peace, rumours of leave—legends of death and miracles of chance.

Most popular are the legends of the immorality and stupidity of officers—and a number of these are not rumours.

*

Finally, at three o'clock, disembarkation starts. A choppy swell has risen and we must go over the tall side of the ship and clamber down the wildly swaying scrambling nets, into the tossing barge below.

It is a heavy climb with the full weight of equipment on your back. Your arms creak in their sockets and the net bucks like a steer. And your mates still on deck, and those already safely down, jeer and cheer as you ride the wild ropes and stumble into the barge.

Dick the Barber is the last man down for our barge. We have to drag him off the net by force. He is white and shivering. Shells don't worry Dick so much, but heights terrify him. All the way over Kokoda he crossed those little vine and log bridges across the ravines on hands and knees, clinging like a koala.

The barge swings away from the ship's side and turns for the land amid ribald jeers from up top and obscene warnings of improbable fates in store for us ashore.

The section moves into the row of tents nearest the beach. The area had been a Yankee cemetery. The coffins were dug up only a few days before the battalion moved in and the area smoothed over with bulldozers.

Slapsy Paint, our Loot, appears and gives his usual vague directions about bedding arrangements and meal parade and wanders off again.

The heavy, leaden-grey casks of the Yankee dead are stacked over in one corner of the area. There are several hundred of them. A gang of American negroes, half-naked and glistening in the sweating sun, are loading them onto lorries.

Pez and Janos go down together to collect their bed boards from the dump near the temporary kitchen.

Jonesy, the thin cook, is idly inspecting the contents of blackened dixies ranged on the long trench fire. From time to time he pumps with his foot the roaring petrol burner that sprays a long, pent blue tongue of flame down the trench.

Pez sniffs hungrily: 'What's for dinner?'

'Stew,' says Jonesy. 'A good bully beef stew.'

'Well,' says Pez. 'If it's good you know what to do with it—a good thing never hurts you.'

They trudge home through the black sand with their bed boards and wooden support frames. Home...a word that means many things to a soldier. It can be a two-man tent in the scrub or a hole in the ground.

Those rows of tents in the naked square still have an unlived-in quality. The dirt on the floors is not even trodden down yet. There are none of the appurtenances of living that make a home—the food box in the corner, the water buckets outside the door, the blackened home-made billy for the inevitable brew of tea.

Everyone starts the business of settling down to a new home—according to taste, once the first scramble for a bed is over. Dick the Barber has the story of the coffins—Harry Drew has been to the 'I' section up the road and has the good guts about the Fourth Battalion—Laird has located food among the wreckage of the deserted American camp down the beach and has marked out a wire and sentry protected ration dump over the other side of the road for future reference.

The coffins belong to the Yanks who were killed taking this beach. They are taking them back down the coast and planting them until the war is over and then taking them back to the States.

'Why the hell don't they plant 'em and let 'em grow,' growls the Laird. 'Another piece of dirt's no different the way they are.'

'It's respect for the dead,' says Deacon. 'Don't you know the dead have to get more respect than the living?'

'Respect this bloke, then,' says Pez. 'He's through living.' Pez had been scraping the sand smooth underneath his bed and uncovered a thin-boned skull and a few frail ribs.

He tosses the skull into the middle of the tent and Fluffy grabs it and checks the teeth: 'No gold. The Yanks have cleaned him out before.' It was the first time Fluffy had ever handled a human skull. 'I'll take it home for me kid sister,' he says. He handles it gently as he passes it on.

Janos examines the rib bones: 'They're so thin.'

The Laird grunts: 'There's not much to a man when you get down to the bone.' Deacon made to pass him the skull. 'Don't give me that,' the Laird rumbles. 'I've seen too many.'

Deacon balances the skull delicately on his extended palm and addresses it with wry heroics: 'Alas, poor Yorick...'

'A swim! A swim!' the cry goes up. Clothes are flung off hurriedly and there is a dash for the tent flap.

Pez gathers the skull from Deacon's hand as he goes and tucks it under his arm. Fluffy tackles him as they race across the sand and Pez, as he falls, tosses the skull to Janos with a smooth rugby pass.

The bunch of lean, naked figures race, shouting, over the black sand to the surf. The bleached skull passes among them, tossed like a football.

Janos, on the fringe of the scrum as they near the water, misses a pass and the skull curves out in a slow arc—hits and rolls slowly until it fetches up against the shell-shredded stump of a coconut palm.

They leave it there and race on—poise for a moment on the firm, sea-washed sand of the beach—then rush down the shallow, shelving water of the ebbing wave and hurl themselves, yelling, over the white foaming wall of the incoming breaker into the deep, cool silk of ocean banked behind it.

Back in the tent Deacon drags out his airmail pad, sharpens a stump of pencil by slitting the wood away from the lead with a long thumbnail, lays tobacco, papers and matches handy, and disposes himself to write his letters.

'Come on down the Yank camp,' the Laird urges.

'I've got to write a letter,' objects Deacon.

'Hell, you can write any time,' the Laird argues. 'But if we don't scrounge through the Yanks early, all the best munga'll be gone.'

'I've got to write a letter,' insists Deacon. 'I've been trying to write it for a week.'

'Another day won't matter then,' reasons the Laird.

'But it's to my Queensland heeler—my Sheila—my best sort.'

'Then she's probably out with a Yank,' the Laird argues conclusively. 'Another two days won't matter.'

Deacon tosses the pad on his bed as he rises to go out.

'Beloved Margaret,' it opens with a little flourish.

The rest is blank.

It is a time of waiting and speculation, rumours and legends, old tales told of old campaigns, endless poker games with greasy, dog-eared packs of cards.

Discipline—the petty, stupid discipline of a base camp—largely disappears. The officers are not so insistent on being saluted at every turn—not that they got saluted at every turn when they did insist on it.

But still the daily bumble of routine orders harasses us.

For three days blankets must be folded in two to the centre and packs placed directly behind them on our beds. Then, for four days, webbing equipment must be laid out on the blankets with the bayonet pointing down. For six days after that the order is changed and bayonets must be laid diagonally across the webbing. Then the order is changed again: webbing equipment is moved down in front of the blanket and the pack must be placed in the centre of the blanket.

These ridiculous orders are an eternal mystery to the troops.

Dick the Barber supposes that the skulls must earn a living and justify their existence in some manner.

Every morning and afternoon there are route marches in the blazing sun with full packs.

They are brokenfoot marches. For a start our feet are tender from shipboard. And the air seems light in the tropics—it leaves empty aching spaces in your lungs after you have been marching a while. The pack straps cut deep into your shoulders as you march and after a few hundred yards you are panting like a fat poodle. The sweat squirts from your skin, saturating the jungle green shirt and slacks.

The only pleasure in it is to stumble in from the march and line up with your dixie at the cookhouse for a quart of tepid, sweet tea—you suck at it, blowing like a horse, and feel it soak down inside of you.

'I think you're being too hard on them right off,' Doc Maguire told Connell.

'Too hard, hell!' said Connell. 'I'm going to march them till they start to drop. Anyone that can't stand this pace won't stand the going further up. I don't want any weak sisters—I want them hard and tough and hungry when I take them in.'

'You can march them in the morning for one hour, Cliff,' said Maguire. 'There'll be no route march in the afternoon.'

They were standing beside the table in the RAP tent. There was no one else in the tent; but young Cliffie, the orderly, who was painting the dermatitis on Brogan's backside in the adjoining tent, heard what was said.

Connell stopped for a moment as though he wasn't sure what he'd heard.

'What the hell do you mean?' he said.

'An hour in the morning, Cliff, no marching in the afternoon,' said Maguire calmly. 'You'll break those men if you keep on running them like you are—you won't harden them, you'll break them.'

'I'll march them how I want.'

'Not while I'm the Doc, Cliff.'

'Keep to your lousy pills—that's your job—mine is to make these men ready for the track.'

'That's my job too, Cliff.'

'I'm the Colonel!'

'I'm the Doc, Colonel.'

'Not when I'm through with you, you won't be,' snarled Connell.

The thin red veins had sprung into a scarlet web on his white face. He picked up a thin glass beaker and smashed it on the table: 'Like that you'll be—from tomorrow!'

Connell was on his way out of the tent. He couldn't have heard, but the Doc murmured to himself, almost with a quiet certainty and satisfaction: 'An hour in the morning—none in the afternoon.'

After a while the Doc came into the tent where young Cliffie was practising his impressionist art on Brogan's haunches.

'How are you, lad?' he asked. 'How are you feeling?'

There was something new in the Doc's voice—he really sounded as though he cared how a buck private was feeling with the island itch around his backside.

'Not bad, Doc,' said Brogan.

Brogan had never before called Maguire anything but 'Sir'—with politeness as insolent as was safe.

Next day we marched for an hour in the morning—there was no march in the afternoon.

A good deal of the day we surf and sunbake naked on the sand. Soon we are nearly as brown as the native boys.

Equipment is checked and issued. We line up at the grindstone in the pioneer tent and sharpen our bayonets—they're handy for opening tins.

Rations are pretty light on at our cookhouse but we live well by scavenging on the Yankee rubbish dumps down at the old camp and by raids on the ration dump through the barbed wire.

The Yanks always seem to have too much of everything—compared to us—and they always seem to leave half their gear behind them when they go.

Down past the point there are hundreds of jeeps and trucks and amphibious craft rusting in the Yank car park. One company dumped twenty good jeeps in forty fathoms of water out past the reef because they had no one to hand them over to and they didn't want to take them with them.

There is good scrounging down at the old Yank camp. Rubbish is piled up in the deserted mess huts and kitchens—shattered crates and boxes seem to have been hurled together in a pile in the middle of the floor. Some of the tins have busted and are rotten, but most of them are quite good. Anyway we always listen when we puncture the tin to make sure the air sucks in and the vacuum seal still holds.

Scratching around the camp one afternoon, Pez and Janos found themselves caught between sundown and darkness in the mess hut. It was a strange feeling—suddenly the light was grey and the beach was desolate. Everything seemed very silent, as though there were watchers in the fringe of the scrub and in the shadows of the sand dunes.

The flywire door, torn off its hinges, flapped mournfully against the wall. It was some distance down the beach to their own camp—the tents were out of sight. No one was visible on the beach—it might have been the end of the world.

'What the hell are you running for?' grinned Janos as they went back down the beach quicker than was really necessary.

'That place didn't feel as though it liked having me there,' said Pez.

The Yank rations are so good that even their rubbish dumps have better food than we've got in our kitchens. Every tent is crowded now with tins of pineapple and peanut butter and assorted stews and hashes. In some of the field rations there are cigarettes and glucose lollies. At night we drink American coffee and munch American-issue chocolate (made in Australia, but not for us) and puff American cigarettes.

There is a deal of discussion about the Yanks. They are all right—they fight well, when they can throw a couple of hundred tonnes of high explosive into a position. They live too well—compared with us, that is. They get too much money—compared with us. They talk as though no one else was fighting the war. They take our girls. 'Over-dressed, over-paid, over-sexed and over here.'

All that's left of them here now is the sustaining rubbish dump of their food, and after a few days the Laird passes the general judgment on that: 'It's all right,' he says, lifting his nose from a dixie of American corned beef hash and baked beans. 'It's all right for a change, but it's too sweet and too soft. For the track—for the hard road—give me our old bully and biscuits. You'd go further on a tin of bully and a packet of dog biscuits than you'd go on a hundredweight of this stuff.'

Things are pretty quiet here.

Only one night Regan gets frightened by the shadows on the beach during his guard. Dick the Barber comes on as his relief. Dick comes up softly through the sand without him hearing and when Regan looks up and sees this figure standing beside him he drops his rifle and runs screaming along the beach.

We found him a couple of hundred yards along where he had fallen in the sand and couldn't rise again for terror.

We got him back to the tent and Pez feeds him the quick cup of coffee Brogan put on. The Laird and Harry Drew are quietly recalling how frightened they've been from time to time by shadows: 'I would have screamed then,' the Laird recalls, 'but I couldn't.'

Doc Maguire walked into the tent. There was a moment's silence and no one seemed to know what to say.

'I heard someone,' said the Doc. 'Young Cliffie told me it was down here—I thought somebody might be hurt.'

'No,' said Pez. 'Just one of our blokes got a bit of a scare and gave a bit of a yell—he's not hurt.'

The Doc was looking at Regan where he sat huddled on the bed: 'Fear can hurt, too. Are you feeling all right, lad?'

There was silence in the tent and all eyes turned to Regan—some things a man has to say for himself.

'Yeah, I'll be OK, Doc,' managed Regan.

'I thought maybe he should come up to RAP for the night. We could send him to sleep, make sure he got a good rest.'

'I think he's better here, Doc,' said Pez. 'I think he's better with us.'

The Doc looked round the tent: 'Yes—maybe you're right.'

There was a long pause. The Doc didn't offer to go. A decision was made and approved by all without a word being spoken.

'Would you like a cup of coffee, Doc?' said Pez. 'We just made a quick brew.'

'Sure,' said the Doc. 'Thanks.'

'Here's a mug,' said Bishie, emptying the dregs of his coffee.

Pez sloshed some water from the bucket and washed the grounds out. The Laird had the billy ready and filled the chipped enamel mug generously.

'Milk?' said Pez, reaching for the condensed milk tin.

'No thanks, Pez,' said the Doc. He sat on the edge of the bed beside Regan and ladled sugar from the biscuit tin container that Pez presented to him with the air of a host.

Medals and strips of ribbon are hard-won things and you can wear them proudly if you have that sort of pride. But there are other things—more common, more generously given, but harder to win—particularly for officers, harder to win. We are brothers, we are men. Our words will never say the things we mean—but living we will drink to you. Dead—our hearts will weep for you.

The Doc sat on the edge of the bed and sipped from Bishie's chipped enamel mug.

'Bloody good coffee,' he said.

The Nip was down the road too far to do any damage to us but you could get the scent of him—that rotten-sweet incense smell he left behind him in the jungle.

His burned, shrapnel-pocked trucks stood along the side of the road—under some of them a crumbling skeleton. Rusting iron push-carts, jungle carts, were scattered round in the undergrowth with pieces of rotting webbing equipment. There were scores of Nip rifles—mostly broken and half-burned—and clips of ammunition half-buried in the sand.

There seemed to be a strange foreign significance to all this junk. You never actually thought it, but you felt: 'This was the enemy; he lived here; he used these things. This rising sun laid out in wood, with the heart burned black and dead—this was his cook-fire.'

The enemy is always strange and there is a faint awfulness about the place where he has been. For you can never imagine the enemy as just a man—if you could, perhaps you would never kill him.

The poker game was going one afternoon; Laird was darning a pair of socks and Deacon was contemplating his letter to Margaret, when Dick the Barber stuck his head in the flap and announced:

'They ate the bookie from the Fourth Batallion.'

He was a nice bloke, the Fourth Battalion bookie. He laid fair odds and you could always be sure of the dough come settling day. Not like Scottie of the Second who welshed on a good book and went through sooner than pay—even though he had plenty socked away at home, money that he'd made from the game. A loud-mouthed alec, Scottie had always been. But the bookie from the Fourth—he was a quiet sort of a guy; he'd done a bit of pencilling before the war and set up in business for himself when he enlisted.

A patrol had gone out across the river and run into an ambush. They had two killed and hadn't been able to get the bodies out with them when they withdrew. Next day they attacked and recovered the bodies; but when they got them they found the brains, kidneys and liver had been cut out and slices of flesh cut from the buttocks.

Harry Drew sucked strenuously at the gurgling bowl of his pipe: 'Yes. We struck that last time in the Owen Stanleys—about Templeton's Crossing—up above the Crossing I think it was. We found the bodies with the flesh cut off the backsides and we found fresh meat in the dixies round their cook-fires later on. But whether they were eating it themselves or feeding it to their dogs—they had a lot of dogs with them—we never really found out.'

'I don't think I'd fancy being eaten,' says Janos. 'Not that it matters when a man's dead—but somehow I don't think I'd fancy it.'

'No,' grinned Pez. 'It's sort of undignified.'

Deacon, lounging back on his bed, head propped up on his webbing pack, flicked a cigarette butt through the flap of the tent with careful concentration before he spoke: 'That's a question—how hungry would you have to be before you'd eat human flesh? A question. Myself, I reckon I came pretty close to it that last time. They say it tastes like pork.'

'How would Selby go?' asked Pez. Selby was the fat cook. 'Old long-pig Selby—the man I'd sooner be shipwrecked with.'

'That bookie from the Fourth had a wife and kid, didn't he?' rumbled the Laird from the corner.

'Yeah,' said Pez. 'Two kids.'

The mail finally caught up with us and most had two or three letters. Some of the literary boys had as many as a dozen, but most of us didn't have the stamina to write to that extent.

Janos had two letters—one from his mother and one from Mary. The one from Mary was quite short. He had opened it first. He read it and then put it aside while he opened his mother's letter and read that slowly.

Things were not good at home. His younger brother had been staying out at night. The landlord had been trying to get them out of the house. There was not much money, but his allotment was helping greatly. Where was he? Was there anything he needed? When would he be home? When would the dreadful war finish?

His mother—she was a woman whom he felt he only vaguely knew. Older than she should have been. Sick and broken and defeated. Always on the verge of tears and infuriating in her ineffectual passion to be possessive of her children. They had never known her. They had been alien to her all their lives, although they kissed her goodbye and fled her tears when they went to the wars, and bothered to half-lie to her when they had been out all night.

Janos turned back to Mary's letter and read it through twice more.

Pez looked up from Helen's letter on the other bed: 'Get one from the Queensland?'

'Yeah, I got one,' admitted Janos.

'I'll get the sporting page off you later,' said Pez.

'Ain't gonna be no sporting page,' said Janos. He tossed the letter across to Pez. 'A Yankee marine—she wants to live in Idaho—she sends her love and hopes I'll understand.'

'You understand?' asked Pez.

'Sure! Elementary, dear Watson! A Yankee marine—she wants to live in Idaho—she sends her love—sure, I understand!'

'Snap out of it,' says Pez. 'Helen sends her love.'

'Tell her thanks,' said Janos. 'But the phrase is distasteful to me just this once.'

Helen knew Janos though she had never seen him. Our wives and sweethearts knew our comrades whom they never saw—sometimes they knew them better than we did.

'You weren't banking on her, were you?' Pez asked after a while.

'No,' said Janos. 'I don't bank on anything.'

'There'll be time to look around when we get back—you can do better. To hell with her.'

'It's a long way to go just to look around,' said Janos. 'Even when you know nothing will come of it, it's good, while you're away, to know that there's a door that you can knock on first when you get home. So long as you've got a contact you can feel you're not all soldier—you can be half a man still.'

Janos was still carrying this black mood around with him when he ran foul of Connell in a dirty temper.

Connell hauled Janos out in front of the section and abused him: 'You're not even a soldier's bootlace,' he told him.

Janos was standing very stiff and straight and he answered Connell back though his voice was so low we could hardly hear him: 'We'll see about that after we've been up the track a bit,' he told Connell.

We thought Janos was a moral to go along for answering back but Connell just sneered at him: 'We'll see,' he said.

Janos was still taut with anger when he fell in again beside Pez: 'I'll show him—I'll show the rotten bastard.'

'Take it easy, boy,' muttered Pez.

Later, they lay on the beach, baking in the sun.

'You won't show anyone anything unless you relax and watch where you're going,' said Pez. He was worried. It's bad for a man to be caught up in anger with one idea. He doesn't watch where he's going or what he's doing—he walks into things on the track.

'Sure, I know,' grinned Janos. 'I'm having a tough trot. I'm feeling sorry for myself. In the words of the classics: "Dear Bill—What a bastard!" '

He lay for a moment and then he said quietly and earnestly: 'I will show him though—and to hell with her.'

The natives were coming back from the hills now, where they had fled when the Nips struck this coast. The poorest refugees in the world—refugees in the jungle.

Pez and Janos watched them come down the wide dusty road that curved round the bay.

A tribe moving camp, or on the march, moves in order—the women, bowed against their loads, laughing and chattering—that shrill island laughter—the men striding out and the children running and laughing beside them. Going to work in the mornings or coming home in the evenings, there is laughter and chatter and they will sing—they are together, there is community among them as they move.

But these people moved silently and slowly. Pez and Janos stood on the side of the road and watched them come.

There were about forty of them strung out down the road—incredible skeletons, their black skins tinged grey with sickness and starvation. They were naked except for strings round their middles holding a piece of rough bark or rough-woven grasses to hide their genitals. They carried nothing but sticks to help their walking and a few clutched leaf-wrapped fragments of food.

They were not moving together. Each one walked as he could and the few children, their bellies swollen with hunger, kept close beside their parents and their heads hung down. There was no talk and no laughter.

'The poor bastards,' said Pez. Janos was silent.

At the end of the line was a man. As bone-thin as the rest, he yet walked with a stubborn, savage strength about him and his sunken eyes burned in the hawk-like skull of his face. He carried a thick hollow bamboo stick. He looked up, straight at them, as he came abreast.

'What have you got there, mate?' said Janos.

The native stopped and tapped the bamboo enquiringly, as he looked at them. Janos nodded.

The man squatted in the dust, keeping at a distance from them. He up-ended the bamboo and shook it, watching them all the while. A tight bundle of gold and white feathers shook out. He caught it in one hand and held it up to them, expressionless.

'Bird of paradise,' said Pez. They came closer to see it. 'And Christ, she stinks.'

The skin had not been properly cleaned and was rotten—putrid flesh and long, slender, gold and white feathers.

'How much do you want for it?' asked Pez.

'One and six,' said the native carefully. He pronounced it *one and sick'ss.*

Pez dug into his pocket, pulled out some coins, and offered him a shilling, a threepence and three pennies. The native shook his head: 'One and sick'ss.'

'He wants the right coin, I suppose,' said Janos. He pulled out a zac and tossed it to Pez.

Pez showed the man the coins—the shilling and sixpence. He nodded and proffered the bird.

'Wait a bit,' said Pez. He went and plucked a large green leaf and took the bird on it. The native picked up his bamboo and set off after the others with long, stubbornly strong strides. He clutched the coins tightly in one hand.

Janos cursed and abandoned his attempt to knock a green coconut from the palm by hurling stones at it.

'Hey!' he said to the big bronzed native boy who had watched his efforts for some time with a quizzically philosophical look. 'Hey, what about shooting up the tree and getting a coconut for me, mate?'

The boy looked at him and grinned without answering. He was a big fellow with a graceful, proud body, a spotless scarlet lap-lap twisted around his waist and a scarlet hibiscus tucked in his crinkly black hair.

'Hmm,' thought Janos. 'Doesn't speak English, eh.' He tried to recall what little pidgin he'd picked up from conversations.

'You fellow,' he began, uncertainly but beguilingly. 'Catchem coconut belongem me.'

He paused expectantly. But the boy just grinned at him.

Janos gestured dramatically to the boy, the tree and himself and tried again: 'You fellow catchem coconut belongem me—me fellow givem cigarette. One cigarette—two cigarette—three cigarette,' he coaxed, carefully raising three fingers in turn. 'Go up along tree, catchem coconut bringem me.'

But the boy just grinned.

Then, just as Janos, desperately, was about to try again, the boy spoke. Perfect colloquial English, with a slight American accent: 'I really wouldn't eat them yet—they're too goddam green,' he said. And walked away.

'Christ,' said Janos, retailing the story with great delight. 'I could have belted him in the teeth! There's me battling with the pidgin—trying to get him up the tree after the coconuts and after all that, he turns to me and says, "I really wouldn't eat them yet—they're too goddam green." '

Nearly six weeks we had been here now...six weeks of nerve-tightening expectancy and subtle shaping of the mind for battle and hardening of the body for the track.

We crowded round the sand table with the country sculpted out in miniature and the 'I' Officer gave us the disposition of our own and the enemy forces—reports brought in by native patrols from deep in Nip territory. There were patches of prophetic red on some of the features along the toy shore. We were to know them in time—Bayonet Ridge and that dark gulch where Slapsy Paint would lie dying in front of us through the long agony of a dying day.

We attended lectures on malaria control, hygiene in the jungle, scrub typhus.

Over the road, 'A' Company showed they had learned their lessons well and were prepared.

They had a new sergeant major—a pukka, spit-and-polish type—who had decided to come and get himself a bit of combat glory before the war ended after spending the first four years of it at Duntroon frightening would-be officers.

He tried to pull his Duntroon stuff on 'A' Company. They warned him several times, but he took no notice.

Then one night they caught him in the dark and beat him up. They knocked him down and then kicked him about a bit.

Not very pretty—but it showed that the boys were ready for the trail. This wasn't a pretty business.

Connell called a battalion parade.

When all the companies were drawn up on the sandy square he took over without ceremony and stood them easy.

'Now keep quiet and listen,' he said.

They slouched, leaning on their rifles, and tipped their hats forward to shield their eyes from the glare of the sun. Connell walked slowly up and down in front of the slouched jungle green ranks—turning a little from side to side to include them all as he spoke.

'I want to talk to you, men,' he said. 'This is the last time I will talk to you all together before we go into action. It will be the last time I'll talk to some of you—before we finish this show, a lot of you will be dead.'

'Cheerful bastard,' grunted the Laird.

'There have been a lot of rumours around that the Nip was starving, that he was disorganised, that he had no arms or ammunition.

'I have instructed my officers to tell you, and I give you my own word now, that such is not the case. Some scattered members of his force may be starving and unarmed; but the great mass of his army is intact, well fed and well armed. They have nowhere to retreat to except the jungle and you will find them a desperate and skilful and completely savage foe.

‘We are going to search out this enemy and destroy him! And, in order to do that, we must be more cunning, more skilful, more enduring and more savage than he is himself.

‘I don’t know what you have been taught in the past, but as far as I am concerned, you can forget what they call the “rules of war”. The little yellow bastard knows no laws of decency, or humanity. We’ll have no time to take prisoners—destroy them where you find them in any way you can.

‘This is going to be no picnic. You are fighting through some of the worst terrain in the world and fighting the most savage foe in the world. A lot of you are going to die, but this battalion, if I have anything to do with it, is going to be the best battalion in the divvy.

‘I think it’s the best battalion in the divvy at the moment—and it’s going to stay that way if I have to kill three-quarters of you to do it.

‘This is a hard game and you’ve got to be bloody hard to play it. I won’t ask any man to go anywhere I won’t go and I expect every man to follow me to the end.

‘Any man who hasn’t the guts to go the full distance can take his pack and go now—I don’t want him with me.

‘The only thing I can promise you is blood and guts—and I want to see more of the Nips’ than your own. I can promise, too, that you will eat more regularly this time than you did in the Owen Stanley campaign—there’ll be no ten men to a tin of bully beef a day this time.

‘That’s all I’ve got to say—except to wish you Good Hunting.’

Janos' voice fell clear and casual through the parade: 'When do we go, sir?'

Connell looked straight at Janos a moment. 'I don't know—but it won't be long.'

A challenge had been noted and remembered.

As we marched back to our tents, Deacon was murmuring with mild inanity: 'Before our wedding day, which is not long...'

'What the hell's that?' says Fluffy.

'*Prothalamion*. I think.'

'What?'

'Sweet Thames run softly till I end my song...'

# 3

Remember, we played poker a lot—hour after hour the greasy broads fluttered over the blanket. You could lose yourself. There was no need to think and the money didn't matter much, whether you won or lost—this was no time to think about money.

The brain could not be shaken with vague fears—you could lose yourself in the calculation of two pairs with the chance of filling or the chance of buying a gutzer straight.

'Never try and buy the middle pin to a straight,' Dick the Barber used to say. 'There's men walking around today with the arse out of their strides through trying to buy a gutzer.'

You could sit for hour after hour in the mechanic oblivion and mechanic excitement of the falling cards—even the cramped and aching muscles from uncomfortable positions became part of the pattern—you became reluctant to ease your aching back and legs because that meant leaving the security, the refuge, of this cave of cards—and outside the night is empty.

Soldiers' talk is casually blasphemous and obscene but there's no real offence in it—it doesn't mean what it says, mostly.

They talk about women, of course. They tell lies about their conquests and amorous adventures in Alexandria and Athens—some rapacious Egyptian trollop can become a Cleopatra in retrospect, and an Athenian shop girl is touched with the immortal fire of Helen—or are you sure she was not your Helen? They sacked and plundered more than Troy to tear her from your arms, and she wept when you were leaving, and I doubt if Helen's ancient tears made such bright and bitter rain.

But the fierce sexual torments that the popular novelists attribute to the soldier on the tropic isle are not for us. You don't find them so much in the infantry—not when there's a blue brewing anyway. Those placid, safe and deadly monotonous base jobs are where such fiery worms breed in the brain and bowels.

In the infantry there is the compensation of that strong comradeship that you never get in a base job. There is the simple animal necessity for subjugating all other desires and instincts to the track—the earth is our lover; its dangers and its refuge. There is the strong emotional and physical catharsis of fear and battle.

We think of women, sure; we talk of women; we desire them; but of way back and of way ahead.

The Laird spoke nearer the truth than the novelists when he stretched back from the lantern one night, tossed aside the letter he had been reading, and sighed prodigiously: 'Ah, I wish I was back home with Mumma—I wouldn't complain, even if she put her cold feet on my back.'

There was the usual outburst of bawdy clichés and variations on the theme.

'It's a great sport,' said Whispering John, licking his lips in lascivious travesty. 'The old indoor sport, the horizontal game.'

'Don't tell me you still indulge, John?' said Deacon.

'Why,' said Fluffy with delight, 'a good sweat and a green apple would just about finish you, John.'

'Don't you worry,' sniggered John confidentially. 'I've had my days—I've done the stations of the cross in Paris and had my nose rubbed in the Bowery. I'll warn you: if ever you get to the Bowery don't go putting your head through any trapdoors you might see—you'll get your nose rubbed if you do.'

'Were you ever married, John?' asked Fluffy seriously. 'If you don't object to a personal question, like?'

'I've got an Irish wife in Liverpool,' said John. 'And that's why I've never gone back. I've got a fat white wench in Panama who looks for me still. And I'd have married a brown girl in Manila—but her husband turned up first.'

The Laird stretched back on his bed and boomed to the world at large: 'Time for a brew! Who's putting the brew on?'

'I'll light the fire,' said Bishie. He swung his feet down off the bed, tossed his paper-backed thriller, *Death in the Dog House*, into the appropriate trash box in the middle of the tent and yawned.

'Best go up and scrounge some petrol from transport,' said the Laird. 'Scorp will give you some—say I sent you.'

'Is there any wood?' Bishie wanted to know.

'No wood,' said the Laird. 'We'll get some petrol and make a dirt fire.'

'Someone get the water,' said Bishie as he went out. He tripped, as he always did, over the fly rope of the tent, and his good-natured curses faded down the line.

Dick the Barber looked up for a moment from the poker hand he was studying in the corner of the poker game: 'I've got the supper: tinned snags from the Yanks and Selby gave me a loaf of bread—you'll just have to cut the mildew away from the edges.'

'I'll get the water,' said Regan. He laid down a letter he had been writing, crouched over a stump of candle on a box in the middle of the tent. 'Where's the billy?'

'The william can,' directed the Laird from his relaxed position on the bed, 'is under Pez's bed. There's no water here, but there's a bucketful under the flap of the first Mortar tent at this end—if you go up quietly they'll never know you took it.

'And now,' said the Laird. 'We want someone to make the toast and heat the snags—a reliable man we want. What about you, Cairo?'

Cairo left the card game he was watching in the corner: 'Yeah, I'll make it,' he said. 'Where's the stuff?'

'Outside in the box the bread and snags,' the Laird issued his communiqué. 'And there's some margarine in the tent next door—ask Ocker for it if you can't get it without him seeing you.'

Cairo paused at the flap of the tent and looked at the Laird: 'What the hell are you doing in all this?' he asked.

'Me?' boomed the Laird. 'Good God, if it wasn't for me there wouldn't be any supper—I organised it.' He settled back on his pillow.

The card game went on. The table was a blanket spread on two cases of .303 ammunition. The lamps were two empty jam tins filled with rifle oil scrounged from the Q store, with pieces of tent rope threaded through the centre of the lids for wicks. They had been made under the Laird's directions and gave a fitful yellow light and a thick curling tongue of black smoke. All the card players spat black for a month after they got rid of those lanterns of the Laird's.

Notes and silver were scattered on the blanket in front of the players and they sat crouched on boxes and buckets. Dick the Barber shuffled the cards with swift, neat flicking movements of his well-kept fingers so that they whispered and rippled as he ran them. It was a smooth shuffle, of long practice—a gambler's shuffle, a cardsharp shuffle—and pretty to watch.

Not that Dick the Barber ever cheated at cards, but he'd learned the art when he was a young bloke and used to play with the crowd from Clancy's gym out in the old back room behind the stadium. Banker Orville taught him, and Banker knew more about shuffling cards, but Banker never took money from a sucker—unless the sucker thought he was smart, and then he took it off him just for the good of his soul and to teach him a lesson.

Old John had left the game once already tonight after being beaten three good hands running by young Griffo. He had taken himself for a walk up around the orderly room. His stomach and back were aching from the discomfort of his box seat and his mouth was stale and bitter with nicotine from the constant, nervous smoking.

He had felt an impotent fury at himself, for losing the bets and for showing his anger. Old John wanted to be liked—he had a great hunger for friendship and affection. But his small soul could only ape the words and gestures of it.

They were probably talking about him now. 'Old John always squeals when he loses,' they'd be saying.

Young Griffo would be counting his winnings and saying in that calmly sarcastic voice of his: 'Hell! If I'd known he was going to whinge so much I'd have given him a quid to stop the game from breaking up. I've a good mind not to play with him again. I don't like a man that can't lose.'

Old John couldn't stay away long. He wandered back to where the remnants of the game were playing cribbage. He wandered up, carefully casual, and watched their play for a while with a small slavey grin. The brown leather of his face was drawn tight over the gaunt bone and his forehead was bald to the top of his head—a skull face.

There came a break in the play and old John moved back into his seat and sat grinning in what he meant to be a pleasant fashion but which had something of the quality of a dog that has been kicked but still wants to be friendly.

He grinned, showing dirty teeth, and said in a hurried, confidential whisper: 'I borrowed a few shilling up the road—what about we go back to poker again, eh?'

'I'll run 'em round for deal,' says young Griffo, flicking the broad around face up to each player. 'First jack.'

The Laird finished his last bite of toast and rich, greasy pork sausage.

'Yeah,' he said. 'This bloke had gone away and here's this orchard heavy with fruit. Well, we think. It's a pity to see those poor citizens in the city deprived of their vitamins. So we borrow a horse and dray and slave for a fortnight—taking the stuff by night and casing it up and freighting it away.

'About ten days later we get a letter from the Market Board. There's no cheque, but a little note that says, "Dear Sir," it says, "We have disposed of your consignment of apples but the return was insufficient to cover the cost of freight and we enclose a bill for ninepence which represents the balance of the freight charge. Trusting you will forward this amount by return mail, we remain, yours faithfully..."

'Yeah, we worked for a fortnight for less ninepence.'

The Laird was remembering that shed at Ginty's place where they stacked the fruit—working by the flickering yellow light of a hurricane lamp which stained the warm, sweet darkness of the shed.

He sank gently, and aware, into the warm flood of memory...the thin, sappy smell of sawn pine from the boxes and the mellow, ripe smell of the apples, and Ginty giving them a hand—his slow, amorous voice, a voice that licked its lips and savoured the words with earthy lasciviousness—as he told the story, the long anatomically detailed story of a generous-bodied French prostitute he had lived with for a week in Paris during the last war. It was Ginty's only story and he had been telling it every night—any time Ginty talked for more than five minutes he started to tell the story or else started to complain about his wife who was tall and thin and mean with herself.

Ginty was dead now—a tree had fallen too soon under his axe.

Regan held up his book but he wasn't reading.

This would be his first time in action. It had always been the same for him—this fear of being hurt and fear of people knowing...

When he was only a kid, his father was trying to teach him to swim out to the reef where it ringed out about fifty yards from the shore, making a smooth pool in the surf. The 'Blue Hole' they used to call it.

'I'm going to teach you to swim, son,' he said. 'The same way as my old man taught me.'

He picked young Regan up and threw him as far as he could out into the smooth water. And when the child came to the surface choking and crying:

'Go on! Swim! Swim!'

But the child floundered in terror, choking and crying, and was half-drowned when the father finally dragged him in. And later, when they got home, old Regan gave the kid a thrashing, a cold-blooded thrashing, for being a coward. Old man Regan had fear in his heart, too.

So Regan lay very still and thought of all tomorrows. Desperately he wanted to be accepted as one of these casual, hard-bitten men—as they appeared to him. But all the time the fear was gnawing at his bowels and he was afraid it must show in his face.

That was why he gambled and lost all his money. He wanted them to say: 'He's a good gambler, Regan!' And he talked big and casual about rackets and brawls. He wanted them to say: 'Regan knows how to take care of himself—he's been around.'

He tried to imagine himself in action—tried to imagine what it would be like from what he'd heard...

'We're cut off,' the Captain says. 'Someone's got to try and get back through the valley, but I'll say it straight—it's a hundred to one shot if you get through. Anyone take it?'

No one in the battered little group stirs. Then Regan gets slowly to his feet and settles the sling of his Owen on his shoulder. He draws deep on the stub of his cigarette and flicks it away deliberately. He rubs the back of his hand across his bristly chin.

'I'll go,' he says casually.

He tried to imagine himself on a lone patrol...or leading a bayonet charge on a hill...

But always in these imaginings there came the moment of pain. And although he couldn't conjure the feel of lead or steel biting into his flesh, he felt the numbing terror in his bowels—the same dazed, blind terror he had felt when he was a child smothering in the smooth water.

And he thought desperately: 'What will I do? How will I know what to do?'

He tried to wipe the dreams away and concentrate on his book. But after he had read a few lines the print blurred again and the pattern began to weave over.

An odd line kept turning in his brain: 'That was a long time ago and in another country...'

It was a line he had read somewhere, or a line Deacon had used, but he couldn't remember—at school, maybe...

Young Snowy from the orderly room stuck his head in the tent. He was wearing a large mysterious grin. 'Sergeant Pennyquick, your presence is requested at the Company orderly room...but quickly.'

There was a babble of questioning: 'What's on? What's doing, Snowy? What the hell is it this time? Is it the move?'

Whispering John tossed down his hand: 'Deal me out until I find out what's up.'

Snowy lingered a moment after John was gone: 'This is it,' he said, grinning significantly. 'I'll drum you—pack your bags—this is it—that's all I'm at liberty to divulge.'

'This is it—this'll be it,' said Bishie. 'Now's the time to say your prayers.'

'Praying'll do you no good,' said the Laird. 'If your number's up, it's up—that's all there is to it.'

'Oh, I wouldn't altogether disbelieve in the power of prayer,' said Dick the Barber.

'I remember a lass called Bertha—a big lass, beef to the ankles, but a hell of a nice kid. Her father used to run the Four Square pub down the 'Gong. "Big Bertha" we used to call her.

'She was always good for a round of drinks on the cuff if you ran short of change and she was always good for a bite if you were short of a quid. Her old man had a couple of dogs and used to train them down on the back track where we ran ours.

'Well, this night Bertha and I went out to the dogs at the Park and there was a dog called Poppies Pride in the fourth that she reckoned was a moral. She had a bad trot in the first three races and up comes this Poppies Pride event. She slaps every cracker she's got on this Poppies Pride and borrows a quid off me and slaps it on the terrier as well.

'Well—the red light's showing and away they go. A broken-down hound that hadn't won a race since Christ was in short pants—a hound by the name of Bigfoot Bill—scarps to the front. And, as they come to the straight and down the field, there's Bigfoot Bill looking a cert and about ten lengths behind him Poppies Pride flat to the boards and the rest of the field nowhere.

'Well, Bertha, she's jumping up and down and screaming for this Poppies Pride to come on! Come on!

'Then, of a sudden, she stops and sits down quiet and clasps her hands and looks at Bigfoot Bill and says in a gentle voice, sort of reverently: "Fall, you bastard, fall."

'And the next hurdle Bigfoot Bill runs slap bang into it, falls arse over head and breaks his neck. Poppies Pride romps home and Bertha collects and I get my quid back.

'So, I wouldn't altogether disbelieve in the power of prayer.'

Cairo, the Log and Fluffy sat together on the edge of the end bed, facing into the darkness towards the sea.

'You won't find it so bad,' the Log was saying, quietly. 'You'll be frightened—everyone is—but you'll get through it. You go through it with your mates, you rely on them, they rely on you. The worst is the loneliness—not so bad in the jungle, but down the desert—when you're moving forward under fire, strung out in a thin line five yards apart, you get awful lonely. You find yourself edging over to the bloke next to you—it makes you feel better to be close to someone. But that's a bad thing—keep scattered, keep apart all the time, then if they get you they only get one—if you're together, the whole group cops it.'

He nodded his head towards the crowded tent: 'They'll fight well, these boys...'

'Hell, there'll always be wars, Harry,' said Janos for argument. 'It's in the nature of man.'

'Then change his nature,' said Pez.

'Is it the nature of man?' demands Harry Drew. 'Or is it the nature of those who lead him, of those who sell and buy?

'Is it man's nature to destroy himself? To shut himself away from all the comfort of the world? Think! Think! While ever there are a hundred million people in the world who parrot like you that war is man's nature—that wars will always be—then there's no hope for us. There's enough blindness and treachery in the high places without ordinary people turning to hatred and stupid cant.

'There's probably not one of you really knows what he's fighting for. You never think! All you can do is parrot that there'll always be wars. It's only by chance that you are fighting this time on the right side. It's just that man is really good at heart, that injustice stirs him to anger of itself, that he will fight for liberty by instinct. Man progresses despite himself—out of a thousand, million blundering years...'

'But we progress,' insisted Pez. 'We progress.'

'Sure, we progress,' said Harry. 'We have done wonders! We have conjured new life, new states, new miracles of machines from the earth and air since the century turned. But how much faster, how much further, could we go if you and all the other millions like you realised your power and fought for that?'

'But you can't do without the moneyed man,' said young Bishie evilly.

'Can't do without the moneyed man!' snarled Harry Drew in disgust. 'How long will it take you mugs to realise that the moneyed man can't do without you?'

'Now, now,' said Janos soothingly. 'Don't do the nana. Take it easy. Keep your shirt on.'

'I'm not doing the nana!' yelled Harry Drew. 'I'm trying to drum some sense into your bloody thick skulls.'

'Gentlemen!' said Whispering John, ducking in under the tent flap.

There was a sudden silence and he looked at them with an important malignant grin: 'Now you new blokes are going to get your feet in the mud. It's on—we're moving tomorrow.'

Everyone felt that faint thrill of coolness in their hearts. No fear, but a tightening of the nerves, a tension of the breath.

'Is it the right drum?' asks the Laird.

John gave his cunning little wink: 'It's on all right; we move to the river, relieve the Fourth and then push on.'

Deacon slowly closed his pad. The page had his number, rank, name and unit at the top. Then 'Beloved Margaret,' and the rest was blank. It was a hell of a hard job to write, that letter.

Everyone was very casual about it—carefully laconic. For the old soldiers it was another move—there had been plenty like this before, they knew what was coming.

But the new men could sense the breath of the unknown and mysterious enemy—the shadows of the long green shore—and violence and death they did not know but had often dreamed about.

Everyone was very careful—the cards fluttered over the spread blanket—there was time for a hand or two of poker yet, and it was not till tomorrow that they started down the long green shore.

# 4

We took over from the fourth battalion and camped that night on the banks of the river. The sections were ringed out in perimeter.

We cut poles and erected our tiny two-man doover tents—straight, strong poles for the stretchers we carried, and these frames lashed onto the bearers with jungle vines.

'These are the best damn thing the army ever got out,' said Dick the Barber. 'Remember how it was the last time—sleeping on the ground in the rain?'

'Yeah,' said the Log. 'That first night at Templeton's Crossing I slept sitting up in a hole with my groundsheet wrapped around me. It rained all night and the water was up to my waist. And my Christ, I was hungry.'

It was a complete blackout that night, of course—no fires, no smoking, no talking after dark. Though you could get a smoke by crouching under a blanket to light the match and you could puff away safely if you shielded the glow of the cigarette at the bottom of the slit trench.

We stood to in the shallow, hastily dug weapon pits at sunset—stand down half an hour after dark. Fifty per cent security—two hours on guard, two hours off.

In the two hours in the pit your eyes ache from the strain of darkness. The night is alive with nerve-sharpening rustlings and cracklings and a million cicada voices of insects, whistling and chirruping and strumming.

There was a sudden, terrifying flapping of leathern wings from the branches above.

'Flying fox,' whispered Harry Drew to young Griffo who was on guard with him. 'Pigs!' he whispered a moment later as there came a steady, stealthy crackling from the bushes in front. 'You've got no chance of really seeing or hearing anything unless they walk right on top of you.'

Occasionally, during the night, there was a shot from further down the line. 'Just nerves,' Cairo Fleming reassured Regan who crouched beside him.

Once there was the heavy boom of a grenade and a long burst of machine-gun fire.

About two o'clock the rain started dredging down. Some of us had not yet learned the tricks of making a dry bed in the jungle. The rain came in and filled up the canvas of our beds like a bath.

The Log squelched as he turned over in his bed. 'Christ,' he said. 'I'll be glad when it's day and a man can get up out of this.'

'Tomorrow we go over the river,' whispered Regan from the bottom bed. 'The Nips are on that side. I don't care if it never breaks day myself.'

'Forget it till tomorrow,' said the Log. 'Get your sleep in, boy—you'll be needing it.'

It was that night after the rain started, remember, that young Darky was killed over in 'B' Company—his mate, Big Brown, killed him.

Big was on guard and Darky, coming to relieve him, missed his way in the darkness and came up on the wrong side.

Big was taken by surprise and swung the bayonet before Darky could speak. It took Darky in the throat and he was dead in a couple of minutes.

They had to tie Big Brown with ropes to keep him down—he was crying and screaming all night—and next day they had to pump him full of morphine before they could move him back.

Four days we stopped there—expecting every morning to cross the river. We learned a number of things in those four days. We learned to fix our doover tents so that the rain stayed out—or most of it, anyway. We learned what saplings were best for bed poles and which would crack suddenly in the middle of the night and flop you into the mud. We knew now for certain the sounds of the flying fox and the pig in the darkness. We learned to wake the instant a comrade's hand touched our shoulder to take over guard. We learned to drop back to sleep immediately we crawled back into bed.

On the second day the sniper fired from across the river.

It was such a matter-of-fact thing—just a flat report from the trees across the river and half an ounce of lead smacking into the trunk of a sago palm near Captain Baird's head.

Such a small thing, but its effect was swift and vast and subtle. It was the final catalyst that changed the chemistry of our brains.

All their drill and preparation had turned to this—all the hours spent round the sand table and Connell's plain words and lectures on malaria and typhus and booby traps and cover and concealment all fused now into a tangible thing. The jungle became hostilely neutral—we couldn't see where the Nip was. This ground, these trees, this river, was no longer our encampment and our home. We were here on sufferance only—we walked only where we could, by chance or force of arms. Without any words being spoken we were drawn together and became brothers against this first shot fired on us—we were on the trail.

Pez and Janos were sitting beside their doover tent on the lip of the river bank when the shot was fired. They rolled into their weapon pit—instinct throwing them there before reason—and in that same scrambling moment all other movement along the bank was gone. Not a man was to be seen—but the jungle held its breath and the leaves of the trees had a thousand eyes.

'I think I know where he is,' said Janos after a bit. 'See that small light green bush against the dark green? He's somewhere about there.'

'Seemed about there,' agreed Pez. 'You can't see him?'

'Think I'll go and get him,' said Janos after a while.

'They'll send out a patrol,' said Pez. 'Don't be a fool.'

'I'll go by myself,' said Janos. 'I got reasons.'

Pez turned to him: 'You haven't got any ideas...because of Mary?'

'Hell, no,' grinned Janos. 'She's not troubling me—it's the other reason.'

'I'll come with you.'

'Because of the reason, I want to go alone.'

'Greta bloody Garbo,' said Pez. He thought for a moment. 'OK. But be careful, boy.'

'Sure,' said Janos. 'I'll be careful.'

They wriggled back out of the pit and slipped round the back of their doover, squatting near the head of their beds.

'We'll move this doover back a few yards, later on,' said Janos. 'She's too open. Lend me your rifle, will you? An Owen might be too short for this job.'

He took up Pez's rifle, snapped the bolt and checked the loading of the magazine. He tied a cloth bandolier of ammunition round his waist and picked up a couple of primed grenades. He straightened the pins so they could be pulled more easily and stuck the grenades in his belt.

'I'll cut down the back and around to cross the river,' he said. 'Give me three minutes and then tell Bairdie I've gone. He'll tell Company and Battalion so they'll know I'm over there.'

'Good luck, boy—you bloody fool. Be careful,' said Pez.

'Sure, I'll be back,' said Janos.

He moved away through the trees. The rifle was tucked under his arm as though he was going duck shooting.

Pez watched until the trees hid him, then went and told Bairdie. Bairdie cursed and rang Battalion.

For three-quarters of an hour Pez lay in the shallow weapon pit where he had lain with Janos. Janos' Owen gun, loaded and cocked, lay in his hand; its nose poked through the bamboo camouflage. He watched the other bank, as two hundred other pairs of eyes watched through the leaves.

His eyes were fixed on the light green bush—but the jungle was blind and still. His ears were tuned to catch impossible sounds—a jungle boot cat-stalking five hundred yards away, or a green shoulder brushing like a shadow through the green tracery of the undergrowth.

It came suddenly and the sound of it was anti-climatic to the drama: a single heavy report and then, a few seconds later, as though the hunter had paused to take careful aim, another report from the same rifle.

'That was ours,' said the Laird.

'Both of them,' said Dick the Barber. 'Both ours.'

'I'll lay a spin that was Janos,' said Regan, as though his wager could intimidate the gods of chance and his own fear. 'A spin that was Janos—I'll bet he gets back without a scratch, even.'

Twenty minutes later Janos re-crossed the river. They were all there to give him a hand up the slippery bank. Pez could only say: 'You bastard—you silly, dumb bastard!' over and over again.

'I'll be back in a minute,' said Janos.

Pez went with him down the track to Battalion.

Lieutenant-Colonel Connell was standing near his tent talking to the Egg Eater—the red-headed Major, and the Adjutant—Winnie the War Winner. Pez stopped on the edge of the clearing and Janos went on. Winnie and the Egg Eater seemed to withdraw as Janos walked casually across the clearing and it was as though he and Connell met alone.

'There was a sniper across the river,' said Janos quietly. 'I got him.' There was the faintest possible emphasis on the 'I'.

Connell looked at him for a long time. 'Good!' he said.

Janos turned and walked back to Pez and they went together down the track to their Company.

Later when they were gathered around Janos, talking it over, Regan looked at him with admiration.

'Jeez, you're a cool customer,' he says. 'Doesn't anything frighten you?'

Janos grinned. 'I was shit-scared every step of the way,' he said.

We went forward on the fifth morning. We knocked down our tents and loaded our packs. We were to leave them at the 'Q' Store before we crossed the river.

'They'll be bunged up to you tonight,' they told us.

'Yeah,' says Dick the Barber. 'If we're still around to need 'em.'

Pez folded his tent in half and strapped it on the back of his pack. Janos had his gear ready and was sitting on his pack reading a greasy, much-thumbed edition of *Huckleberry Finn*—a Yankee service pocketbook edition that he had found down at the first camp. Pez checked round the doover to make sure nothing was left behind.

'This your shirt?' he asked Janos, holding up a piece of muddy green.

'Yeah,' said Janos. 'But throw it away. I've got one and that's enough for any man on this trip.'

Pez bundled the shirt up and tossed it away out of sight in the bushes. Suddenly he felt a twinge of irritation.

'I dunno—I think you ought to carry it—means you haven't got a dry change.'

Janos looked up slowly from his book. 'How many shirts have you got?'

'One,' said Pez.

'Well, what the hell's all the excitement about?'

'Jesus,' muttered Pez, half to himself. 'The stuff we throw away—you could outfit three armies on it. Someone's got to pay for it.'

'Well, take it easy, boy,' says Janos. 'Take it easy—no need to snap my head off.'

'Sorry,' grunted Pez.

He struggled into his equipment and pack and lay down on the comparatively dry ground that had been sheltered by the tent. The pack slid high up on his shoulders, under his head, to make a pillow. His rifle was lying across his body and the brim of his hat was pulled down covering his face.

When you slide down on your pack like that you can feel all the weariness and the small aches of your body settle down into comfortable leaden sediment in your bones and it would be good to lie like that forever.

Pez's eyes drooped, half-closed under the hat brim. They were heavy, burning a little, and pebbly from sleeplessness. He could feel his lips hot and dry—there was a taste of blood on them—and he could feel how the skin had tightened over his cheekbones.

But these things helped too, he realised. They were somehow in character, part of the rhythm, and they helped you to play the part of a soldier. That is the only way—to try and identify yourself with the jungle and the pattern of war. To become the animal that steps quietly and is sensitive to the flutter of movement or the whisper of alien sound, that can sleep in the rain and suck enough strength from an hour of sun. Withdraw, conserve yourself. There is no yesterday and no tomorrow. Time is the time of war or the time of peace. Gather your strength for the job in hand and keep just one small core of your brain where you can remember, without urgency and without despair.

There was still Helen and this problem.

Bob should be home on leave now. Would she tell him this time? Would she change her mind about waiting till the war was over, and tell him? How would you tell him? Would you just say: 'Oh, by the way, Bob, I've been bouncing around with Pez while you've been away. I love him. I've decided to divorce you and marry him.'

And what would Bob say about it?

'Oh, all right, dear, I'll have my things out by tomorrow night.'

Maybe that would be the way if people were intelligent and civilised—or if they were peculiarly inhuman in their emotions, and decadent. But there is nothing inhuman in the way you feel for Helen—it seems right that you should love and be together.

It's hard to imagine how Bob feels about Helen. Could

he feel the same way you do? It always seems impossible that other people's blood should run as warm as ours and their hearts ache as deeply.

Did a man have a right to take another man's wife away from him? Or maybe you're forgetting that, theoretically anyway, wives don't belong to husbands any more. Maybe it was up to Helen—it was up to her to say yes or no—not for you or him to wonder if you had a right.

Funny thing—you'd known her for years before it happened—never thought of her that way before. It started that leave—she'd been unhappy and lonely and you'd been bored—too much grog and not enough to do. You'd known her since she was a kid—always been good friends—never thought of her like that before.

It started off as just a roll in the hay—and a damned good one, too—but it soon changed. It soon became...Hell! It was hard to put into words, except that it seemed good and right and proper to be together.

Well, the problem was still there and still unanswered. But there was an unreality about it from here—from this angle of the jungle slanting under the brim of a slouch hat—you couldn't work it out from here...

Janos was shaking him heavily by the shoulder.

'Come on, boy, come on...Time to move—it's on for young and old.'

Half-asleep, Pez scrambled clumsily to his feet under the weight of his gear—shrugged the weight of the pack into a more comfortable position, slung his rifle on his shoulder and climbed into line behind Janos. Janos turned and grinned.

'How you feeling, mate?'

Pez grinned back. 'Better,' he said. 'You know, it's a good thing we don't both get dirt on the liver at the same time.'

'Right, three!' called Harry Drew. 'Drop your packs at the "Q" Store as we pass.'

The section filed out and slogged down into the mud of the track.

You lie beside the track and watch them go. You lie with head and shoulders resting on your muddy pack, rifle resting across your body and your legs sprawled—the soldier rests where he can. (See the little red book.)

They come up tall and brush past you in a swish of green as they go. You see them from the dramatic perspective of the ground beneath their feet—the brass studs shining in the soles of the heavy jungle boots—the Yankee gaiters laced round the calf of the leg—the stained jungle-green slacks and shirt open at the neck—the rain-battered slouch hats slanting over one eye.

They come with their rifles slung over the shoulder, their Owens cradled under the arm. They lean slightly forward—their shoulders hooded against the weight of the pack—a cloth bandolier of ammunition slung round their waists—a couple of primed grenades stuck in their belts—a tin of bully beef and a packet of hard biscuits in their pouches.

Identification discs are tied round their throats with old bootlaces or pieces of cord and dangle on their breasts like crucifixes. A soldier's crucifix—meat tickets they call them: dead meat tickets.

They move along the track in single file, dumping their packs in the clearing on the bend, and pass on, stripped down for the trail.

Cairo Fleming, as he comes up level with you, grins and says: 'Get off your back, you bludger.'

And you just grin back and say: 'Good luck, mate—I'll be right behind you.'

'Get one for me, too, Fluffy,' says young Onnie Smith, who is cleaning a Bren gun in the pit beside you.

'Get one yourself,' says Fluffy. 'There'll be plenty to go around.'

They go past and on—down to the river...

The river should have been clear. We had patrolled it every day.

But you can't trust the jungle—comb through it if you like, it is clean and safe, you say—but even as you pass, ambush may be gathering behind you, or in the trees above you.

They let the scouts go through and the head of the section reach the bank. They opened up when the body of the section was strung across the river.

Brogan died swiftly in the middle of the stream. He fell and his body was dragged away by the current. Young Griffo, acting stretcher bearer, forgot the bullets, as a man will do, and went to do his job—which was to help Brogan now he was hit.

But the current, as it twisted Brogan's body around, let his shattered head drift to the surface for a second. Griffo could see there was nothing for him but burying. The time for that was later. He bent again for the bank.

It was a solitary machine gun. The bullets came pattering over the water like recurrent bursts of hail. There was a horrible dream quality about it. You couldn't, in that moment, imagine that these drops falling in the river, skipping like stones, were really deadly. You couldn't tie them up with a phantom gun that was beating—stopping—beating somewhere a thousand miles away.

Oh, this is death and fear and ecstasy—and the lungs, and eyes and ears are filled enormous with the colour of it. The drill books don't provide for this. The instinct for the earth and cover is helpless here. We are caught in the horrible grey catalepsy of the rushing river.

There, on the bank, a thousand miles away, is life—there is the earth, our Mother, that we can embrace her—the sweet mud; the sheltering furrow; the strong protecting arm of trunks and trees.

Here we are naked in the empty plain of the river. This is no home—the earth we know, but here we are alien, rejected and exposed to the black rain. Our limbs are held in a leaden dream—we hurl ourselves for the other bank but we go with the horrible slow motion of a dream—and all the time the bright deadly rain is pattering around us in the river.

And yet we are not afraid.

This has been too sudden, too monstrously improbable, for fear to develop. All the chemistry of fear is working for our salvation—the adrenalin of fear shoots in our blood, firing a tremendous strength to fling us to the shore.

Before you feel true fear you must realise, you must be aware. The protecting dream-film disappears and you are seared with the burning brand that sends you screaming and helpless, fleeing—or with the corruption of fear that numbs you and leaves you helpless, trembling, transfixed.

Suddenly this obscenity flops on Regan's brain and he starts plunging through the water with a horrible bucking motion—like a terrified horse trying to drag itself from a bog.

It's funny in a way. It's almost funny.

Fluffy is laughing at him—a shrill, unnatural sound in all this roaring soundless tumult.

Harry Drew is yelling from the bank: 'Come on! Come on! Come on!'

The innocent, pattering rain runs across the water and patters over Fluffy's body. He is still laughing—he drops his rifle—it splashes into the river—he is holding his stomach with both hands—laughing or screaming—he staggers on—laughing or screaming. He falls as he tries to run up the muddy bank—his hands still under him, holding his stomach—he twists his head sideways out of the mud—the mud is in his mouth, but he is still laughing—or screaming...it goes on and on. The sound goes on and on for a thousand years and we are caught in the grey nightmare of the river—we are shod with lead and clothed with iron...

Regan has fallen near the bank and Harry Drew is dragging him up from the river. Regan is crying—sobbing. Harry throws him into shelter against the trunk of a tree and turns for Fluffy. But Griffo reaches him first.

He is lying as he fell—his legs dredging in the water, his arms under him, his head turned sideways—laughing out of the mud that mires his mouth. The bank is running red under him—the blood runs down and is licked away in the foam of the current.

Young Griffo is tearing open the first-aid pack as he hurls himself through the water. He seems to move faster than any of us—he is doing a job for someone else.

He turns Fluffy over.

The kid's still sort of laughing and hanging on to his stomach—his fingers are spread wide and stiff but it's coming through them—his hands are muddy and bloody—his eyes are open. His face is still sort of laughing but his eyes are open and wide—and they know.

Griffo tears Fluffy's shirt down and the wounds lie open.

'Oh, Christ, Christ, Christ,' Griffo is saying over and over. He scrapes the mud away from Fluffy's mouth.

'You can't do anything for him,' snarls Harry Drew.

Fluffy's laughing turns to moaning and soon he will be screaming.

'Knock him out!' snarls Harry Drew. 'Hook him! Hit him! He's finished—put him out! He'll die before he comes to—don't let him suffer.'

Griffo looks up. He is white.

'I can't,' he says, 'I can't hit him.'

Harry scrambles over, snarling at him, but he groans when he looks at Fluffy.

'Poor bastard—' he says. 'Poor kid.'

He smashes his fist against Fluffy's jaw. The jaw snaps shut. Fluffy's body slumps. He is silent.

The blood still runs from him, staining the jungle green of his trousers black. It is running into the hostile river—licked up and flicked away in the alien current.

We should all have died in that river but, by the normal miracle of war, we survive.

Brogan is dead. Fluffy is dying. Young Sunny, the drag man, turned back and made the other bank, though with three bullets in one thigh. The Log has a bullet burn across his shoulders—Griffo goes to him.

All the others are safe. They have vanished—blended and gone into the silence and the jungle and the dripping leaf.

Old Whispering John is there, crouching against a stump, his eyes fixed on Bishie crouching ahead of him. Old John's dirty teeth are showing in a fixed little grin. The webbing pouches on his chest are riddled, and there are even bullet burns on his shirt. Later he is going to show them and boast about them: 'How's that, eh? The old soldier gets through, eh?'

'Funny,' he'll say with ill-concealed gloating. 'Young Fluffy, his first up and he cops it, and me, the old soldier, I walk right through it with not a scratch. Funny, eh?'

Harry Drew sends a swift whisper into the silence of the trees: 'Laird, take over for a while—watch Pez and Janos.'

The whisper goes from tongue to tongue in leaf and branch and fern.

Harry Drew slides round the tree and flops down beside Regan: 'How are you feeling?'

'OK,' shivers Regan.

Harry puts his arm around the kid's shoulders—thin shoulders.

'Come on, kid—everyone feels as bad first time. Will you come with me—stick with me?'

'Sure, Harry,' says Regan.

Sure, Harry! You are God, here on this muddy track, if you can beat these wasps of wrath away—if you can walk like Christ and unafraid—if you can keep me from death—or, better still, if you can keep me from fear of it showing in my eyes. Sure, Harry!

Harry Drew leaves the tree in the peculiar crouching crab-like run of the soldier under fire. He pauses by a tree, dodges on and falls into the shadows of the shrub. A few seconds later Regan follows him with a valiant imitation of that same run. He pauses faithfully by the same tree, dodges on and falls panting heavily in the shadow of the same bush a few feet from Harry Drew.

'OK, kid?' says Harry.

Regan manages to grin through his parched lips.

'Sure, Harry.'

# 5

But we must be inconstant to the earth—there's the pity and the terror of it. We must rise—and never more reluctant from a lover's bed. A red cross is drawn on a map and we must go there. The sky is grey and the jungle crouches, bland and waiting. The wet drips incessantly, implacably, imperturbably from the leaf—charting the passage of eternity.

Pez and Janos crouch against the bole of a tree and talk it over. They crouch on their haunches, crouch on their toes—ready. They do not look at each other—they watch the jungle. They whisper from the corners of their mouths. The rifle and the Owen are held loosely in their hands—ready.

'They might open with mortars,' insists Pez. 'It'd be a hell of a thing to walk into your own mortars.'

'They won't,' says Janos. 'They'd wait for us to call for them—and we've got no line back across the river. They know we're here somewhere. They wouldn't use mortars unless we called for them. We've got to get that gun.'

'They might just open up.'

'The longer we wait the less chance we've got!'

'Where do you reckon the gun is?'

'About three or four hundred yards down—can't be far from the bank.'

'They might be strong.'

'Probably just a gun crew.'

'They'll know we're here.'

'We know they're there.'

'Wait a while—we might get mortar support.'

'If it doesn't come in thirty seconds, it won't come till we call,' says Janos.

He turns his wrist and glances briefly at the second hand of his watch. He keeps his wrist turned and his gaze goes back steadily to the jungle. Thirty seconds. The leaf drips fifteen grains of eternity.

'OK,' he says. 'Bring them forward, not too close. When I give the hand, get them down and let them keep down—less movement the better. They'll probably have a cover man out—you watch him—I'll try for the gun.'

Janos glides away. Pez follows—his hand conjures the patrol from the earth—they materialise, drifting through the grey-green of the undergrowth. Harry Drew leads again, Regan is close behind him.

Here is a ballet and a symphony—here is a dance whose name is Death—whose overture is silence—waiting on the cue for savage strings, the bowel-plucking whine of the bullets. All the earth and yesterday and tomorrow are blotted out in this fierce, relaxed concentration that narrows a burning spotlight on this rain-soaked stretch of mud and jungle. The earth is suspect, save where we stand—the trees are treacherous—the leaves slant like eyes.

Janos drifts...the Owen in his hands loses the stock of metal and plastic and becomes an instinct of life, shifting and probing like mantis antennae...

Pez's hand beats imperatively towards the earth and the furtive life behind him returns to the earth.

Janos drifts on. Pez follows—his dominant hand keeps the earth still and unbreathing behind him...

Janos was right. They had a cover man out. Pez killed him as he fired at Janos, and Janos sprang towards the pit where the two Nips were trying to swing the gun around against him.

He killed them both in the pit. One fell forward over the gun. The other—a big fellow with a square face—was trying to clamber out, trying to run. He fell against the edge of the pit, his crucified arms stretched up over the mounded earth, his fingers clawing, and he was biting in agony into the red clay of the edge of the pit when Janos fired again—and passed swiftly on, to drop, crouching, into the shelter of a further tree, his eyes swift and steady on the jungle as he snapped another clip into his Owen.

In a few moments Pez joined him.

'I went through these two Nips in the hole,' said Pez. 'Nothing on mine at all. Three pens, a watch and a bundle of yen notes—take what you want.'

'Not for me,' said Janos. 'Thanks for getting that first one—he'd have got me.'

'I didn't,' said Pez. 'I just nicked him. He tried again when I came up to him. I brained him with the butt.'

The lobe of Janos' right ear was a bloody smudge. Pez saw it as he rose. 'I'll fix that for you,' he said.

Janos rubbed a quick hand against it; stared for a moment at the smudge of blood on his palm; then rubbed it off on his trouser leg.

'She'll do,' he said. 'Let's wander on.' He took two short steps, vomited briefly and spat with a wry mouth. He glided off into the trees.

Pez looked for a moment at his loot from the bodies. He stuck the watch in his pocket, tossed the notes and fountain pens back into the pit and followed Janos.

Behind him, the patrol materialised through the trees.

The rest of that day we see nothing of the enemy—but that is no safety when with every step he may appear. We pass down the track. We reach a spot on the map, marked with a cross in red. We camp.

We eat a mouthful of bully before dark. Our water bottles we have filled on the way. The rest of the Company is following behind us, spread in a thin line down the track back to the river. We dig ourselves in before dark and a quick patrol clears our front without finding anything. We make ourselves beds of grass and branches, and huddle under the thin shelter of our waterproof capes—but the rain comes through. It is impossible to stay dry or get warm. Hour on, hour off, we are on guard. When your turn comes, your mate nudges you and you open your stinging eyes, hold your rifle a bit closer and crouch, listening for sounds you could never hear. It is impossible to see. No one sleeps much that night—or the next—or the next.

That first night, before dark, Connell had come up the track to see us in our forward position.

Janos stepped deliberately onto the track in front of him.

He held up two fingers. 'Two more makes three,' he said.

'Good,' said Connell. But he paused before he said it.

'Good work, boys,' he said to the rest of us. 'Damn good show. I'll try to get you up a hot meal sometime tomorrow.'

He went back down the track.

Janos stood by the side of the track, his arms folded, and watched him go.

Days and weeks followed—quietly enough, but never with peace. The enemy is unpredictable. For days we probe through country where a handful could hold up an army—but never a hostile shot is fired against us. Then, suddenly, we will stumble on a machine-gun nest, or a sniper in some hopeless position where the only retreat is death.

But always, whether we are forward or in reserve, there is that small fraying—continuous and never ceasing—on the nerves.

You who know war in a romantic dream, or in the sob stories of newspapers, might imagine that it is only the thunder of bombardment or the terrors of the charge which breaks a soldier's will and manhood; but the slow-burning acid of monotony and sterile days can be as bad, or worse. You live constantly with a small fear that can never be spoken, and never become real, but can never be dispelled.

You might know you are safe—you are behind the lines—there are no Nips within a quarter of a mile. You might know that, but the knowledge can never fully soothe the nerves or stop them from trembling as antennae to probe the blind bank of the jungle to the side of you, and the edges of the clearing where the jungle path turns. Too often, death has come out of the silence and the unliving jungle. Though you might know there is no danger, it is no use telling your body and your nerves and the dark places of your brain so long schooled and skilled for the task of being ready for death and violence, when all is still.

So you have no rest. The shadow and the smell and the texture of death is always real and tangible about you. Walk ten yards into the scrub and the nightmare closes around you.

All seems still and silent. Then, as you stand, you are aware of interminable life—a vast, corrupt writhing as of slimy sea-flowers and forest washed forever by a drifting ocean. Nothing is still. Every leaf and twig and branch and bud writhes and quivers with some secret, malignant life of its own. Everything crawls and curls on the stem. Nothing is silent; that hush you heard when you stopped you now find is made up of ten million tiny, rasping, whittling, evil sounds—all of deadly portent if you listen—

Did the twig break, or was it broken? Did the bush rustle, or did the stealthy footfall brush it?

There is an eternal smell of death and decay. The silt of centuries of corruption is trodden moss-like underfoot. You grasp a branch and it crumbles in your hand like mushroom. The leaf and the plant and the limb are always dying and are swiftly eaten by the savage and unhealthy organisms that live.

The earth itself is vile and stinks with the essence of corruption long distilled into it. And for this desolate and savage and unwholesome earth, men died...their blood stained it and the sickly sweet smell stained its vileness deeper.

'Why are we fighting for this?' the Laird boomed. 'For my part, let the Nips keep it—serve the bastards right!'

Deacon asked Connell one day when he met him, ploughing down a track ankle-deep in mud.

'I was here before the war,' said Connell. 'There's an old saying—where there's mud there's money.'

There is only the time of war and the time of peace—this is the time of war.

We are forward section for days. We drop back and another platoon moves forward through us to take up the spearhead. We go forward again.

There is a rhythm about the track—a material music about the ache of the pack on your shoulders and in the pulsing muscles that go on labouring long after they are exhausted beyond the point of normal human endeavour.

There is poetry in the feeling of the rifle stock under your hand, or the Owen cradled over your arm. There is kinship between you and these finely machined pieces of walnut and steel; there is strength in them. A man who, unarmed, would scratch the earth, can face the enemy like a knight of old with a lance couched on his arm. As a musketeer felt for his sword, so we feel for our guns. Not that we love them as individuals—one gun is just like another—it's just the feeling they give you.

You get sensitive to the feeling of the earth under your feet. There is the slide and dragging weight of the muddy track and the lightness of firm, sun-baked earth when you strike a hard patch.

Your skin runs oily with the drenching sweat of your body and there are those incredible moments when, by chance, passing through a glade or coming out on the side of a hill, a blessed breeze comes for a moment and the sweat freezes on your body in ecstasy.

The body is a good machine and will keep going. The knees are the worst. They tremble violently—'laughing knees' we call them. When you are moving it's not so bad; but when you stop you find your knees are giggling and you stand under your pack, shivering like a beaten animal...

So the days go on. We march—the dull slog through the mud or sand, when the only horizon is the earth and the heels of the man in front of you, and the weight of the pack bows you down as a load of sorrows. We carry—returning swiftly and lightly over the track we have taken and dragging crates of ammunition and cases of food back with us to the front. We advance—stripped down to the ultimate burden of hard rations, ammunition and weapons—armoured with the sensitivity of fear—holding chance as a talisman against mortality. We fight—occasionally the scattered or the single shots—the body falling, the scream of pain or the frightened whimper; sometimes under the thunder of big guns, locked in combat on a savage hill.

Old Whispering John gets thinner and darker each day. His little bright blue eyes burn deeper into his skull-like face. He never loses his little grin—but it seems fixed, as something apart from himself.

Younger men and tougher men physically than old John have cracked up and been sent back sick, but old John goes on. Each one that goes, he sniggers with evil satisfaction: 'Another one gone, eh? Another of the young colts cracked up and the old soldier still going, eh?'

Sometimes he hobbles and falls back a bit on a long march—but he always catches up. He's never in the front, he never leads, but he's never exactly behind; and all the time he sniggers with satisfaction: 'The old soldier keeps on going, eh? The young blokes crack up and the old soldier keeps on going, eh?'

John's darkening complexion doesn't come altogether from the sun. He gave up washing the day we moved up to relieve the Fourth and the nearest he's come to it since we crossed the river is when it rains extra heavy. John gave up cleaning his teeth, also, and it gets so that we avoid him when he comes up and tries to buttonhole us confidentially.

'Stinking Jesus,' Deacon calls him privately.

'Even his best friends won't tell him,' says Dick the Barber.

*

Our Company was spread along half a mile of beach that ran from a small river to the edge of a large clearing. On one side was the pebble-white, sharply shelving beach; on the other, a grey stretch of swamp. The wood sprouted between and the main body of our troops were sprawled through the thicket. Most of them lay in the hot shade, with head and shoulders propped up on sweat-stained packs, rifles lying close at hand and legs sprawled ungainly.

About ten-thirty the Nips opened up with a barrage from their mountain guns in the hills. The Log prodded the sleeping Cairo Fleming as the splintering explosions of the shells strode on long legs down the fringe of the wooded strip, probing into the blindness of the trees. These ordinary contact shells couldn't do much harm, but occasionally the Nips sent over a timed fuse that burst in the air and the shrap smacked down through the trees. They were nasty.

Cairo yawned and slid down into the hole beside the Log. They crouched, listening for a moment as the shell bursts strode past them down the beach.

Cairo's head drooped and he was about to drift into sleep again when a shrill, moaning scream swelled up from down the beach—swelled and rang on and on—and the cry was flung from mouth to mouth along the beach: 'Stretcher bearers! Stretcher bearers!'

The scream of the wounded is the loudest sound of battle—even through distance you can feel the minute texture of its agony sliding like ice in the veins and the pity of it like a strong hand twisting your bowels.

Doc Maguire passed them, going towards the

screaming, ploughing through the sand on the fringe of the trees.

'Who was it, Doc?' called Cairo.

'Don't know. Don Company, I think,' he replied without looking or pausing.

The line of shells was creeping back down the beach now. You could see the burst of them in the sand and the violent, lopped convulsion of branches where they struck among the trees. Maguire walked straight into them without slackening.

'A good man,' said Cairo.

'Yeah,' said the Log.

A few minutes later the grapevine whisper ran down through the line: Rocky Bennet—burst right on top of him—dead.

'He was a good little bloke,' said Cairo. 'Remember that time in Cairns he took on the three provosts? He did three months in Groverley for that lot. Remember, he always used to say: "Three months'll do me, I'll do it on my head. A month for each of the bastards is fair enough." '

'Was he married?' asked the Log.

'Yeah, I think he had a wife,' said Cairo. 'I think he got married on that last leave.'

They sat for a long time in silence. The Log crouched there—his head sunk on his breast, but his eyes wide and steady with memory.

'What are you thinking about, mate?' asked Cairo.

'Nothing. Just thinking,' said the Log.

'Anything worrying you?'

'No,' said the Log. 'I was just thinking that if my son had lived he'd be about ten months old now.'

Cairo looked quickly away and there was silence in the pit.

All day long we huddle in the trees. We are waiting for our guns to come up within range.

Way back behind us, the Gunners and the Fourth Battalion, which is in reserve, are bringing up the guns. They tie ropes and chains to the twenty-five pounders and drag them along by animal force...straining and groaning inch by inch through the treacherous soft places—cheering and laughing breathlessly as she rumbles slowly but steadily behind them on the good going. Chanting the Volga Boat Song breathlessly. The Volga, not so Vulgar.

The old catch-cry is raised, of course. The old vulgar suggestion is made: 'If you're going to work like a horse, you might as well look like one!' A couple of clowns carry the idea further. They expose their genitals and prance against the ropes, neighing and pawing like stallions.

It doesn't make the drag any easier, but it gives a laugh. It helps keep the men on their feet long after they should have fallen.

Janos heard the plane first. The whisper sped and the fringe of trees between the swamp and the sand came swiftly to furtive life—crouched, concentrating on the sky.

The Nips had been shelling us desultorily all day. Rocky Bennet had been killed and Doc Maguire had three or four wounded bedded down under a bank at the bottom edge of the beach.

The Wirraway came cruising casually down the beach, about four hundred feet up, and dipped its wings in salute to us in the trees as it swung inland. We could see the saluting gloved hand of the observer and his hooded, goggled face peering down as he waved.

'Those blokes are mad, you know,' said Dick the Barber, 'plain mad. Fancy going up in the air when there's good solid ground to crawl on.'

The Wirraway circled the hill where the Nip battery was set up. The plane buzzed up and down, casually skimming the trees, and occasionally darting down viciously and peck-peck-pecking at some target. Then she climbed up and circled, waiting, above and back of the hill.

There was a swift, high rushing and whining in the air, and halfway down the Nip hillside the trees exploded and a big mushroom of dirty white smoke puffed out.

The plane came skimming over the hill and banked through the smoke.

A few minutes later, another smoke shell landed higher up the hill. Then another burst, right on the ridge—then another and another, tracing the contour along. We cheered.

'They never miss, those boys,' said the Laird. 'They snipe at five miles.'

The Wirraway dived in again, strafing along the ridge—peck-peck-pecking viciously along the hill—like a willie wagtail attacking an elephant. Then she turned and came sweeping over our trees again, her wings dipping in salute, and sped back down the beach.

'He'll be sleeping warm and eating well tonight,' said Pez. 'We should have joined the Air Force.'

Janos grinned: 'We should have stayed home,' he said. 'Here, have some bully.'

'I'll have just a trifle more of the *pâté de foie*, me good man,' says the Deacon to Bishie.

Deacon is lounging in his pit, his feet propped up on the edge, his hat carefully tucked at the back of his neck to stop the sand trickling down where his head and shoulders rest against the other wall.

'Certainly, old cock,' says Bishie, who is reclining on one elbow beside the pit.

He digs a knob of pink and white bully out of the tin with a spoon and proffers it to Deacon: 'More *foie gras*, me Lord—and would your Lordship care for an iced vovo to go with it?'

'Thank you,' says the Deacon, taking the knob of bully delicately in his fingers. 'But if you refer to the dog biscuits, me good man—stick 'em! I believe I lost my second-last filling on one this morning and my dentist's three thousand miles away.'

'Anything else, old cock?' enquires Bishie servilely.

'Just a sip of the Veuve Clicquot.'

Bishie passes the water bottle.

'And tell Lady Jane to bath well before she goes to bed,' continues the Deacon. 'Last time, me good man, you were a little careless behind the ears—scrub her thoroughly all over this time.'

'Oh, sure, old cock—all over!' leers Bishie.

'And tell the second chambermaid I'll see her in the dunny later,' says the Deacon.

The sun is dying. We are packed and ready.

The barrage opens with a single whine and explosion on the enemy hill.

Then the shells fall—one-two...one-two-three...

And now the air is full to the black sky with the rushing whine, the shuttling, zipping, heart-swelling pattern of shells plucking the heartstrings of the earth and sky. In the gathering darkness we can see the constant flashes running along the enemy ridge and the crown of the hill is smothered in smoke and flame and thunder. The hill top seems to heave and we can almost see dark things tossing and falling...

We move out of our little wood and, in single file, cross swiftly under cover of the first darkness and our sheltering guns. That quarter-mile of waste sand and kunai into the broad shelter of the trees seems as wide as the earth. For the music of the guns—whether they are our own or the enemy's—makes your heart enormous. We are lost for ever with shadows before us and shadows behind us and the sweet foul music of hell above and around us and the naked, sterile and unfriendly earth beneath our undestined feet.

We make the shelter of the trees.

By whisper and touch and instinct we break up into our little groups and bed down in the darkness—huddled closer together for comfort in this strange place.

After a while our barrage eases. But at irregular intervals during the night, one or two shells will burst over on the hill.

'That's just to keep 'em awake and make 'em nervous,' Harry Drew whispers to Regan.

The Fifth Battalion, who are travelling further inland, are coming up to the hill. They are to put on an attack in the morning and the barrage from our twenty-fives opens up again with the first smudge of grey.

Then, quite suddenly, the shells stop. Everybody is listening in that silence. Then it comes—the swift, thin clatter of the Brens and Owens, the heavier beat of the Nip woodpeckers, the spaced reports of rifles and, smacking through them all, the slamming explosion of mortars and grenades.

'They're into it,' says the Laird.

All day long the firing continues on the hill, dying away for a while into silence spaced by single sniping shots, then flaring up again in the swift rattle of automatics and the slam of grenades.

We hear it, fading a little behind us, as we advance that day, and it is still with us when we camp that night.

We lost a man that night.

Early in the afternoon we passed along the beach where the trees were twisted with the mighty winds sweeping in from the depths of the Pacific. They were things of violence—with great roots widespread, clutching the earth, and limbs twisted paralytically to withstand the storm.

Charley Company was along the beach, Don Company was across the track, and we swung inland, into the fringe of the dripping rainforest, to make the other side of the perimeter.

We had a bit of time before dark and we made ourselves comfortable. We put up our tents carefully and made our beds strong. They sent us up a meal in dixies from the kitchen back down the track—bully stew and dehydrated spuds boiled up. It was fairly hot, it tasted good, and there was even some fairly fresh bread that had been dropped by the bully beef bombers back in the clearing.

It looked like being a quiet night, but the rain and the wind started about a quarter of an hour after dark. The rain came dredging down through the thick curtain of trees. The wind could not touch us, but we could hear it beating gigantically against the treetops.

It was an old, dead tree, shaken and felled by the fist of this wind that, in the middle of the night, crashed onto the doover tent where the Deacon and Bishie dossed with the Log and Cairo Fleming.

Another four feet to the right and they would all have copped it. As it happened, Bishie was sitting up near the head of his bunk to keep himself awake for his guard. The tree missed him, smashed the end of his bed and, falling at an angle, killed the Deacon as he slept.

Most us didn't know what had happened. Some of us, near enough, heard the crash. We heard the sound of chopping—axes beating on solid, dead wood—but in this blind world of wind and darkness and drumming, ceaseless rain you can't tell where things are. You can only sit tight and watch and listen. What happens in your own tight circle of rain and darkness is all that concerns you—the rest can wait.

It took an hour to cut the tree away from the Deacon. It had crushed him across the chest and stomach. He couldn't have felt a thing, he must have died straightaway. They had to lift carefully to get him onto the blanket.

The Log and Cairo and Bishie dug his grave. Bishie wept while he dug. They buried him just after dawn.

A soldier leaves so little when he dies—a watch they gave him when he left the office to enlist—a small pack of faded photographs—some old letters in a mildewed wallet—stained with the sweat of his skin when he was living and the blood of him when he died.

As we passed out on our way down the track that morning, the grave was by the side of the path, the fresh-mounded earth with a sealed, inverted bottle stuck neck down in the soft soil. Bishie had lashed together two small broken branches from the tree that killed him, to make a cross.

Oh, Deacon, who sought love and never found it! If I had paused beside you as you dreamed, as Fluffy did that night on the boat...I wonder did the ancient mark burn on your brow then, even as you dreamed? Oh, Deacon—to life you should have been so great a lover—but the embrace of the earth is cold and wet where you lie under the rain trees on that little hill.

The telegram that went back home said: 'Killed in action.'

Deacon had carried a battered writing pad in his webbing pouch. Bishie found it as he went through his things and tossed it away. As we passed on, it lay under the bushes in the rain, not far from where he lay.

His number, rank, name and unit were scrawled across the top of the page. Then 'Beloved Margaret,' with a little flourish. The rest was blank.

You get used to the colour and the smell of death—the blood from the mouth, the destroyed flesh, the small black scuttling things that infest the corpse in the jungle.

You get used to the colour of death in the living—the grey jungle-pallor on the faces—the bright, blind weariness of eyes—the bones showing up white and hard under the skin.

After the first time, you get used to a man going crazy beside you—you watch for it. Usually you can pick them—they get very quiet for a day or so—their eyes get an absent sort of look, as though they were thinking back. Then a madness boils up in them like a curse of Job and they will scream and sing with it. They will fight you with the strength of it—clawing with teeth, and boots, and nails—cursing and praying.

And sometimes after you have overpowered them and your blood and their blood is on their hands with the violence of trying not to hurt them, the madness will suddenly leave their savage flesh. They will collapse in your arms like a child and weep with gentle despair while you carry them to Doc Maguire.

Usually when you get them there, the madness comes again and they will shriek for you not to leave them. You will have to hold them while the Doc presses the bright needle into their arm, crooning the while with a gentleness no woman ever heard from him. The strong grey medicine soothes the fever of their blood and abates the wildness of their heart and brains.

We call it 'going troppo'.

Our Company was forward most of the time down this stretch of the shore. Sodden, desolate country it was—desolate jungle. Every afternoon about four the rain would start—you could see it come sweeping down the hills—and it would drench down solidly all night.

Our section was point section most of the time. Janos was point scout and he made himself a legend that sped back down the shore and flew inland to our troops cutting through the hills. He saved us all many times with his skill and swiftness. Ten Nips he had killed, and each time he bailed Connell up on the track and added the score.

'Eight,' he told Connell as we held the marsh on the river.

'Nine,' he said the day after Deacon died. He walked into Connell's tent at the edge of the abandoned aerodrome, overgrown with kunai—'Ten,' he said.

Connell said nothing, but he boasted to others of what his battalion and his men could do.

It was at that 'drome, remember, we had a fine grog party. There was a lot of junk, plane wrecks and equipment scattered through the tall kunai grass. I don't remember who it was first lighted on the compasses filled with alcohol, but everyone was in it. Out came the chipped enamel mugs and the dixies and there's everyone busy cracking compasses, like you'd crack an egg, and draining the spirit.

It tasted fine over the tongue—smooth, like a good Scotch whisky—but about six inches down it started to expand and burn—vodka was mother's milk to it!

Our mob retired for the night as full as bulls. There was considerable indiscriminate firing at an imaginary enemy, and Janos had to be restrained from a project to shoot through the centre pole of Connell's tent so that it would collapse on top of him.

'You remember that time in Syria,' recalled the Laird, 'when big Johnno from Don Company was going to shoot Boomerang Billy. You remember, he staggers along to the Officers' Mess and bellows—"Boomerang Billy, I want you!" And old Boomerang shoots out, ready to fly right up to him. "Boomerang Billy, you bastard," says big Johnno, very solemn-like, "Boomerang Billy, I'm going to shoot you." And Boomerang Billy takes off up the hill, with big Johnno staggering after him, letting go a burst every now and then from the hip. He couldn't have hit him in a year, but Boomerang went up that hill like a mountain goat.'

Good old Boomerang. He had a completely misplaced confidence in his ability to steer a course by the stars.

You remember, too, that day he was drilling us at Kilo 69. You know how officers pick up clichés—esprit stuff—'This is it, chaps,' kind of thing. Well, Billy's was, 'One man spoilt the whole show!' Whenever he was drilling, you could rely on having to do it over half a dozen times because 'One man spoilt the whole show!' This day we'd gone round and round and every time it was the same complaint. When he stopped us again—it was as hot as hell—and he bellowed: 'One man spoilt the whole show!'

a weary voice pipes up from the back row—'Yes, it was you, you silly old bastard!'

Slapsy Paint, our Platoon Officer, rejoined us at the 'drome before we went on to Drogula Bay.

Slapsy had been fairly new to us when we sailed and we hadn't seen much of him since. He was a funny sort of bloke. A big ox-like man whom you'd take to be either lazy or stupid—he was lazy.

He'd been a Duntroon officer for most of the war—but he wasn't the usual pukka-wallah type. He told us once, in a moment of rare confidence, that he'd joined the permanent army long before the war because he was looking for a job. He had been a carpenter, but he reckoned that was too hard and too uncertain, so he joined the army. They had shot him out to us—he didn't want to come. He had been quite happy where he was at Duntroon and quite prepared to finish the war there; but there was some trouble about a major he hooked one night he was drunk in the mess and he finished up with us. He made no pretence—he didn't want to fight. He left the show to Harry Drew and old John and Janos—he just wanted to keep out of trouble.

But he was always running into trouble with Connell. Orders were that sleeves were to be rolled down at sunset and the face and hands smeared with mosquito repellent to discourage the malarial anopheles. Officers were supposed to enforce this order rigidly, but Slapsy himself would be wandering round half the night naked except for a grimy towel round his middle. Connell would come through in his jeep on inspection and Slapsy would wander out on the track to meet him, naked except for the towel round his middle, his big feet squelching in the mud.

Slapsy carried a flute with him and when we were back a bit he'd sit for hours on the edge of the bunk in his doover, the grimy towel round his waist, his muddy feet sticking out in the rain, trying to play the Brahms Lullaby.

It was the only tune he knew, and soon we all knew it—every wrong note as Slapsy played it, every uncertain pause where he started a passage over again. We would grin at one another as the sweet, quavering notes floated up through the trees and rain.

'Jesus, he's at it again,' Pez would crow delightedly.

'I wish he'd get another tune,' Janos would complain.

Slapsy might be pretty drack as an officer, but there was a certain pride and delight in him. We used to boast about him to other platoons and invite them up to hear him playing.

There had been some doubt about the illness that prevented Slapsy from joining us when first we started up the long green shore. But after he'd been back with us a few days, we sort of forgot about that. There was that time they struck the booby traps on the beach—Jimmy Mollison walked into one and had both his legs blown off. They called on Slapsy to come down and delouse the area. He borrowed a makings off Pez—he was constantly running out of tobacco—rolled himself a smoke, borrowed a match, hauled up his pants. 'I'll be back in about half an hour,' he said. 'If you hear a loud bang, I won't be back.'

Slapsy was all right. There are a number of good officers, of course, and a great number of poor ones. The ones that came up through the ranks on the field are generally the best—they know what it's about. Most of the blokes that haven't been in a blue before aren't worth a bumper. We've all got to learn, of course, but most of this batch of Duntroon boys imagine that they know it already—just because they read a book. They're all right in standing camp—they bellow very nicely and impressively on the parade ground and know the regulations backwards—but in a blue they're dangerous with their regulations—you've got to tell them to get the hell out of the way and not make nuisances of themselves.

So we didn't mind Slapsy—he didn't try to interfere—and he's a character.

It was a heavy march to the bay. Not that we struck much opposition on the way there—only one Nip, dug in like a weasel between the twisting roots of a big tree.

Snowy Myers' platoon were ahead that morning and big Tomo had got this Nip with a hand grenade. From what we could see of him in the hole, he was a mess—we didn't search him for souvenirs.

We were carrying full packs, and ammunition besides—mortar bombs and .303. It was just a matter of marching—clambering and sliding and slogging, until your mind is black with exhaustion, and your body aching with the weight of your pack, and your chest burning.

When the word came to halt, Pez stumbled off the edge of the track—dragging Janos and the case of mortar bombs they carried between them. He dropped his end of the case and fell backwards on his pack, sliding down it until his head and shoulders rested.

Gradually...the heart's thunder ceases—the breath eases its labour—the red blood fades from behind the eyes.

Pez sat up, dragged out his makings and rolled a cigarette. He stuck the weed between his dry lips and scratched a wax match on the serrated bottom of the tin. These tins were usually made too smooth, so that the match wouldn't strike—or too sharp, so that they tore the head off. The head tore off Pez's match.

'Here,' says Janos, whose cigarette is going. 'Ignite yourself, my friend.'

Pez leans across painfully and lights his cigarette from Janos' bumper.

'All those as have tobacco may smoke,' says Regan. 'All those as haven't can go through the motions.'

Old Whispering John is talking about the girl he knew in Panama and describing her amorous powers with detailed relish.

Young Griffo is sceptical: 'You tell me that? You think I'm a bunny because I come out of a hole?'

'Man came up out of the mud,' declaims Harry Drew. 'He makes and destroys a thousand cities; and now he flies through the air, drives ships under the sea and has touched the stars! And where does it get us?' His gesture embraces the jungle and the track: 'Back in the mud!'

Somewhere up ahead a heavy machine gun starts beating. There is a momentary silence down the line.

'Woodpecker,' says Janos.

Then comes the smaller, stinging rattle of the Bren and the Jap gun beats again in a long, heavy burst.

There is always someone firing up near the front, but you can never get quite used to the sound of the enemy—a tightness bands around the chest and stomach and the nerves and brain become light and sharp and clear.

After the guns stop, old Whispering John forgets to resume his amorous tale and Harry Drew leaves his philosophising.

'Wonder if they got anyone?' says the Laird. 'That Bren gun didn't fire again—only rifles and Owens.'

'Big Tomo would be scouting,' says Janos. 'He'd be awake.'

'I got a feeling we're going to strike trouble at this bay,' says the Laird. 'It's been too quiet.'

No one disagrees with him.

Myers' platoon had reached the edge of the bay when they struck the woodpecker. Janos was half wrong about big Tomo—he was point scout, but he wasn't awake. They killed him as he slipped from the shadow of a tree and waved his section on.

Five are wounded and we've got to get them back. The barges can't come into the beach until dark, and that's too long. The obstacle is the river about four hundred yards ahead of us. It is not very wide but it's armpit deep and fast, ripping straight through the beach and smashing into the sea. We can't take them any other way—they've got to come over that river. We can't bridge it, but the Laird sends word back and some empty four-gallon drums and some long ropes are rushed up to us. Some of us cross the river—it tears at you like you were chained to horses.

They bring the first of the wounded down the beach. Young Sad Saunders, it is. He's copped it somewhere in the legs. His rifle lies between his thighs and his legs are strapped to it to keep him straight.

'It's OK,' he says. 'It's not too bad—poor old Tomo copped the lot.'

We lash an empty drum at each corner of the stretcher to float it and tie the long ropes, two at each end. We take the two front ropes across the river and the men on that side haul as the others pay out. Some of them go with the stretcher. We manage to keep it fairly straight, but the current drags at it and bucks it against the ropes. The men in the water are fighting against the current themselves all the way and can't help much except to steady the raft. 'It's a rough trip,' Sad groans once, but says quickly: 'She's right, keep her going.'

The black stubble of his chin shows up against the deadly yellow-white of his skin when we lift him up on the other side. He's a bit wet, but all right. The relief stretcher bearers take him over and continue down the beach.

Maguire arrives just as they are taking Sad. He examines him swiftly and lightly: 'You'll be all right, lad—I'll be back by the time they get you on a bed.'

He comes up to the river: 'How is it?'

'Oh, bloody lovely,' says Harry Drew. He shows the Doc our ferry. 'Two hundred Yankee ducks rotting down at the camp there, but when we want one here to ferry casualties we don't get it...we've got to drag them across the river like this.'

'Yes, I know,' says the Doc. 'I know how it is.'

He crosses the river—goes up along the beach to check the wounded they are bringing down and comes back before the next case arrives at our ferry.

'They'll all be pretty right if we can get on to them tonight,' he says. 'Be gentle as you can with them.'

He goes back down the beach with long strides.

So we cursed and struggled across the river with the wounded. Cursing our own inevitable clumsiness with them, cursing the river, cursing the goddamned, bumble-headed brass hats that let amphibious craft rust down on the shore so that we had to hurt these men, already hurt, dragging them across the river.

We get them across. Darby Munro is the last. In the face and chest he's copped it. We can't see much of the face for pads, but his eyes are shining bright with pain and drugs and he tries to grin at us: 'I never did like that nose of mine much, anyway,' he mumbles.

We nearly lost him crossing the river. The stretcher bucked and he rolled half into the water. Pez and Janos were on that side and they got their hands under him. For long, long seconds they struggled, cursing and panting and praying, against the fierce drag of the current—while Harry Drew snarled savage, impotent curses from the bank and the Laird bellowed prayerfully: 'Hold him! Hold him! For Christ's sake, hold him!'

Pez had Darby by the shoulders and he could feel him sort of laughing: 'Ride her, ride her,' he was mumbling through the bandages. 'Drop me and I'll bloody sue you.'

They lifted him back and went on to the other bank.

*

The Nips were dug in solidly at the bay.

For a week we were locked in battle with them on the hill—close, bloody fighting filled with steel and thunder.

The first three days our guns were still too far behind to support us. The fourth day the guns opened up and the moaning they wove into the sky and the shattering explosions in front of us that shook the earth were sweet music. But ammunition was light on—our attack failed—we had to wait another day for the full strength of our guns.

It was about this time we noticed that Slapsy was going a bit odd. He came crawling round the pits. He seemed to want to talk about something—and seemed to have forgotten exactly what it was. He asked odd questions—how we got our nicknames, were our mothers living—and when we asked him how things were going—when the guns could be expected, whether food was coming up to us—he didn't know.

Pez and Harry Drew talked it over.

'I think old Slapsy's going a bit queer,' said Pez. 'Have you noticed him?'

'Might be,' agreed Harry Drew. 'We'd best watch him. He's a big man—it could be awkward here if he got violent.'

'What can you do, Harry, if he goes off his nut?' enquired Regan, who was hunkered down beside him in the pit.

Harry Drew looked at the thin, battered, grimy kid and grinned: 'Stop him the best way you can. If you happen to be around, kid, you'd best use a rifle butt to make sure.'

So we watched him. But it didn't make any difference—it was so odd, so unexpected, the way it happened—it was funny, almost.

Things had been quiet most of that morning—both the Nip and us locked in the earth on that hillside—an occasional sniping shot or burst of automatic fire sweeping the ground. And suddenly, incredibly, the sound of a flute broke the baleful air—sweet and off-key, as always, the Brahms Lullaby. And, fantastically, Slapsy Paint rose up out of the earth—naked except for the grimy towel round his middle—walking in some calm nightmare of faraway—earnestly and absently playing on his flute.

None us saw him until it was too late. It was so unreal, so incredible—he walked calmly up the hillside, playing his flute—up towards the Nips, playing his flute—pausing and starting over again, as he always did, on that piece in the second bar.

Only one of us found a voice. The Laird was shouting: 'Get down! Get down!' when they fired and we saw Slapsy fall—and you could feel the shock, the incredulous surprise in him, as he fell.

The earth saved him—the solid Mother Earth. He fell into her shelter as a drunk can fall safely down the stairs. We could see he was hit—it looked pretty bad—in the legs and somewhere in the jaw or throat.

The Nips swept a curtain of fire down the hill, and we answered back—it was something to do—it was the only thing we could do. The Nips couldn't get to him, but neither could we—there was too much open ground. We could only wait for dark.

Slapsy Paint just lay there, as though he had woken in a strange room after being sick a long while—or being out on the grog. He just seemed to be lying there.

His flute had fallen in the open and a Nip sniper amused himself smashing it. We could see the little pockmarks springing in the ground around it. One—two—three—four—five—six—the seventh shot smashed it. There was a *Banzai!* from up the hill.

Through that long afternoon he lay there. He either couldn't, or had sense enough not to, move. From some of the pits we could see him—from others, as the afternoon deepened, we could hear him.

There is nothing more horrible...to be locked into the earth by lead and steel, and hear, through the agony of a dying afternoon, the moans and cries of a man you know. To hear him, to see him, and not be able to move—to know that no heroism and no millionth chance could take you across that burning gulch to bring him to safety.

He moaned and cried...on and on it went...you couldn't shut your ears to that sound—it seemed to swell somewhere from inside you, yourself, and ring on and on, horribly, insanely, and for ever.

In the pit, Regan shivered with pity and shook his head, trying to writhe away from this evil dream: 'Oh, no!—No!—No!'

'Don't listen!' said Harry Drew. 'Don't listen, kid!'

'Christ, I could hit him from here,' said Janos. 'I can finish him with one bullet. Quick—he'd never know.'

'Might be best,' said Harry Drew. 'He looks bad. It might be best.'

'Oh, no...no...no.'

'You can't do it,' said Pez. 'He might live. We can get him after dark. Put the mortars on and we can get him at dark. He might live.'

Mostly he moaned or cried. The only words we could understand were every now and then he would call out, over and over: 'Leave me—leave me—leave me—' over and over and on and on through that long afternoon.

Pez and Janos and the Laird nominated as three to go and get him when darkness came.

'I know where he is,' said Janos. 'I can find him in the dark—I'd best go.'

'I'll tag along with you,' said Pez.

'He's a big bloke,' said the Laird. 'I guess I'd better make one to carry him.'

'I want to go, Harry,' said Regan.

'Don't be silly, kid,' said Harry Drew. 'There's plenty more to go than you.'

'Harry, I've got to go.'

'He's a big man, kid. It needs more weight than you've got to carry him.'

'I'll carry my end—please, Harry, I've got to go.'

Harry took him by the shoulders—thin shoulders: 'Don't try and play it big, kid—a man can only do as much as he can do—that's all that's wanted of you. You don't have to go.'

'I have to go—I want to, Harry.'

'OK, kid—if you're sure.'

'I'm sure.'

Slapsy's cries stopped just before sundown.

'He might be dead,' said Harry Drew. 'I'm not going to risk men to get out a dead 'un.'

'We've got to go, Harry,' said Pez.

'He's alive—he must be alive,' Regan wanted to say, but he didn't say it.

'We'll go,' said Janos.

The mortars threw everything they had against the Nip emplacements on the hill. The sharp, splitting explosions of their bombs beat along the ridge like hail, until the hill was thick with the thunder of it. From the pits we opened with everything we had—firing on fixed lines to leave a narrow lane of safety for the carrying party to reach Slapsy.

It was nothing, really.

Janos and Pez and the Laird and Regan just climbed up out of the pit. Crouching, they followed Janos, who led them swiftly and surely to Slapsy.

They lifted him onto the stretcher. He moaned a little. They carried him back. He was alive.

It was nothing—to walk in the darkness of that fiery furnace. Just that it was uncomfortable, the trip back—a man seems heavier lying on a stretcher and Slapsy was a big man, anyway. You can't crouch to gain the false security of worshipping the earth when you are carrying a stretcher—you can scramble on all fours, lumping the stretcher between you, but that takes longer and is more awkward in the dark. So they stood up—trusting to Janos to lead them straight back—and stumbled as quickly as they could down the hillside to their own pits.

Harry Drew clasped Regan to him like a lost son: 'Good kid!' he said. 'Good kid!'

So we lay in the earth and waited for our guns to be fed.

We got word back that Slapsy would be right. Doc Maguire had patched him up fine before sending him back down the line. On the table Slapsy hadn't come to properly, but from time to time he muttered: 'Leave me…leave me… leave me…'

We lost Bishie here, too. He had been wounded with a grenade on the second day. There were half a dozen pieces of shrap in his back, but he kept quiet and refused to go down to the RAP for treatment. But after the third day he was so stiff and sore he could hardly move.

Doc Maguire got to hear of it and came crawling up to the platoon. 'Where's Bishop?' he said with a grin.

He went to him: 'What the devil do you think you're doing, still here?'

'I'm all right, Doc,' said Bishie. 'Honest I am.'

'We'll have a look,' said the Doc. He lifted Bishie's shirt gently—it stuck to his back in places. The wounds were shallow, but angry-looking and their blurry mouths cried out.

'Three days ago you got hit?' asked the Doc.

'Yeah, I think it was about three days ago,' said Bishie.

'You know, I ought to put you in on a self-inflicted—you should have come to me when you got hit.'

'I'll be all right here, Doc,' said Bishie. 'Just patch me up now and I'll be all right here.'

'No,' said the Doc. 'You're coming with me, boy—you've had it for a while.'

'Let me stay, Doc.'

'Come on, boy.'

Bishie looked as though he was about to burst into tears when he said goodbye—or maybe it was just not sleeping for three nights. The Nip machine gun was beating over on the left flank. Bishie went to pick up his rifle.

'Leave it, boy,' said the Doc. 'You won't need it for a while—with any luck you won't need it again.'

They crawled out back to the track and the Doc's hand rested lightly on Bishie's shoulder as they went together down the road.

After dark that night, Bishie hobbled down to the beach, round past the headland, to meet the barge that was to take him to hospital. He remembered the last time he had waited on such a beach. A long time ago now it seemed...

After the terror and the flight through the jungle, the terror of waiting—the fear that after all that monstrous effort they should be taken. And then the nightmare journey in the small boat—hugging the shadows of the shore by day—eyes burning and blistered from staring at the sky—watching, watching for the treacherous wings.

And now his wounds were aching—he was tired—deadly tired. 'But at least, this time,' he thought, 'we didn't run.'

On the fifth day our guns opened in strength and the hill flamed and roared and trembled under their barrage. They blasted it like a quarry face—you would have sworn that no thing living could survive in that desolation. We ourselves, when we came up from our safe earth, were blinded and deafened with the insanity of it.

But there were some left. We used the bayonet—it was a savage, swift, unwholesome fray—we won the hill.

We took no prisoners. Only one Nip cried surrender—he came out with both hands raised high, crying something in his native tongue.

The Log killed him with a savage thrust, and kept on stabbing long after the Nip was dead. We had to drag him away.

Of course, the Log had a reason—that dazed scatter of shots from the battered hilltop when we started our attack had killed Cairo Fleming...

The Log sat hunched against a tree on what had been a Nip hillside. He sat with his head cradled in his arms between his knees—his forehead pressed against the rifle in his hands...

'I remember the day that Cairo Fleming died...sure, other men died that day and had died in the days before—but Cairo was my friend.'

Cairo's dead, Log—no ghost will rise to speak for him.

'It's hard to tell you...in my own heart I know my friend, but the things I can put into words maybe won't sound important or impressive—there's no drama, no hero stuff in them. Just that we marched and slept and fought together—were broke together and cashed-up together.

'We got our share of strife and we raised our share of merry hell in Alex and Jerusalem and Haifa and Tel Aviv. Remember that leave in Cairo? That's where he got his name—we acquired a Wog donkey and stormed the front steps of Shepherd's Hotel, demanding accommodation for man and beast as the law provides!

'Maybe we never saw the pyramids, but we saw plenty else—lights and shadows—alleys and arak. Anything can happen in Cairo—and when you're young—and a soldier—and the world's your oyster—it usually does.

'Then came the desert—Cairo and I were there—then Greece...We were there when they tried to hold the Hun on the river at Larissa. But he broke us and the cry was: "Get out as best you can!" Cairo and I took to the hills together.

'After a long time, a dangerous time—through dark nights, by small ships threading through the islands of the Dodecanese—we came out of Greece together.

'Maybe you can imagine what those words mean—*We came out of Greece together.*

'Then we came home—came Kokoda and the Trail—came the long rest—came this.'

We know him, Log. We know him. They pinned no medals on him, they made no speeches—we need no medals or speeches—we know him and remember. He was just a good, ordinary bloke—that's a point—that's an important thing—he was an ordinary bloke like you or me—maybe a bit better than you or me.

Because, you see, Cairo was an Australian—a blue-blood—an Australian of the oldest, proudest stock. His ancestors didn't step ashore with Phillip; nor were they chained below decks in the prison hulks. They were here before Cook—before de Quiros—before the ancient eyes of Polynesian and Egyptian mariners may have seen these shores.

'Cairo was my friend.'

Come, Log. That stinging of your eyes comes from the long weariness of battle—it nestles beneath all our heavy lids. Come, Log. We will bury him on the hill he died for. Come, Log. Let us lay our black brother in the black earth. Mourn not the dead—but always remember: He was black—he fought and died—he was a good man—he was an Australian.

So we possessed the bay.

As we took our hill, the barrage had lifted onto the next. Another Company passed through us and they in turn took their hill and so on.

We possessed the bay.

# 6

Connell was on the phone: 'But my boys don't want it, sir,' he said. 'We can push on tomorrow—they're in the pink of condition.'

'Listen, Connell,' said the Brig. 'We're not in that much of a hurry. They're going to rest whether they want it or not. You'll be relieved tomorrow.'

Connell slammed the handset down and strode outside his tent. He stood glaring around for a moment and then yelled: 'Sergeant Hino! Sergeant Hino!'

The little fat RP Sergeant came scrambling up through the trees and stood saluting agitatedly: 'Yes sir! Yes sir!'

'Get a party and clean the scrub away from around my tent,' said Connell. 'It looks like a brothel.'

'Of course,' Tubby Hino tells us later, 'I thought of an answer to that one—it was on the tip of my tongue to say it too...'

The Second Battalion came through and relieved us. We rested ten days at the bay.

Sickness and battle had thinned us down. That hill had cost our own group Slapsy Paint, Bishie, Cairo—young Griffo with a smashed leg, Dick the Barber with a stomach wound. Old Whispering John had a long, shallow knife slash down his back from the attack on the hill—but it was only a scratch. He sniggered about it with great satisfaction: 'The old soldier gets through, eh?'

Once we stopped the malaria struck us. The Atebrin hadn't stopped it much, though we took the little yellow tablets faithfully twice a day. Harry Drew went down, Regan followed him. We met the Log one afternoon coming down from the hill—he was shivering violently from cold and the sweat was beaded on his brow. Back he went.

The surf was good and Pez and the Laird swam slowly about a mile out to catch a big shoot.

'You're mad,' Janos said. 'I wouldn't go out there for a thousand pounds—it's too dangerous.'

Pez and the Laird swam slowly—climbing up the great, long swells and bursting through the smother of foam at the top. Every now and then when the wave carried too much white on top they duck-dived under it and were dragged down—pounded and smothered joyously under the broken waters.

Out in the deep swell they lay rolling slowly with porpoise delight in the great depth of cool, clean water. There is an odd sense of comfort mixed with loneliness, swimming so far out. It is as though a man drifts in an alien—but not hostile—environment and really only a small grey ghost of fear and loneliness can rise in his mind.

The Laird called softly: 'Hey, Pez! Look over there—do you see what I see?'

A shark was cruising slowly about fifty yards away—the triangular fin cutting smoothly towards them—tacking away—then cutting back.

'Nothing we can do,' whispered the Laird. 'Keep still—and if it comes, splash like hell.'

They watched and waited—the fin cutting away and tacking back—then it disappeared.

They waited—it seemed a long time…

'Come on, boy,' said the Laird. 'Let's catch a shoot in.'

They swam with painful slowness back into the line of breakers. They waited three or four waves until they caught one that broke at the right time.

Like seals on that foaming crest—the wild exultation of speed and foam and spray—the swift rush of swimming to catch the weight of the wave—the gradual balancing of power as you reined on to it and the swelling, roaring rush; flung a long age down the cooling, soaring breast of the wave—closer and closer and closer to the shore where it destroys itself on the broken mouth of the rock—they slide off before the thunder.

Connell went down to the RAP and found Maguire. 'Come for a walk with me, Mag,' he said.

'Just a minute,' said the Doc. 'Try the sulpha on that one,' he told his orderly, 'and make sure he gets back early in the morning to have it dressed again.'

He came out of the tent. 'Where do you plan to take this constitutional?' he asked.

'Let's go along the beach,' said Connell. 'I want to get away from it.'

'From what?' enquired Maguire mildly.

'From this—from everything!' said Connell.

They went down the track through the trees and onto the white sand of the beach.

'This damned sitting still gets on my tit,' said Connell. 'Brig's orders—silly old bastard.'

'Relax, Cliff,' said Maguire. 'You can't keep going all the time—why, anyway? What makes you want to run all the time?'

'We're here to do a job—let's get on with the bloody thing!'

'You're not fighting the war by yourself. Something troubling you, or are you just leading up for me to prescribe a mild sedative?'

'I don't want your pills!'

'What are you afraid of, Cliff?'

'What the hell do you mean?'

'I mean what's worrying you—what's the trouble?'

'Nothing.'

They walked on some distance over the sand in silence.

'What do you want from life, Cliff?' asked the Doc.

'I don't know, Mag,' said Connell after a moment.

The Doc nodded his head and murmured aloud, but to himself—'Sad people.'

When you are sitting still you have time to think—when you think your brain rusts and sheds flakes of despair. It is blind ahead—discontent and self-disgust—run, run—it's no fiend that close behind you treads—it's yourself.

'Most people,' said the Doc, 'are running from something—from the past, the present or the future.'

'I don't need a psychiatrist,' said Connell. 'Save it for a thesis.'

Remember how the old house had stood back deep in the grounds, and the long, gravelled drive that had been a coachway when the house was built? A wonderful drive where a boy could come in through the big iron gates coming home from school at the end of term—drop the suitcase on the grass and run—a long wonderful way with the gravel crunching and splattering under his flying feet—wonderful running with the wind in his face—and there would be Mother standing on the porch waiting, as she always was for him when he came home, laughing and crying and holding her arms out to him as he ran...

There was that soft, secret thing between them—something that instinctively was hidden from Father. Remember those slow solemn walks around the grounds, with Father all sober black and gold watch chain—the Sunday morning walks after Church—with Father discoursing ponderously on Life and Responsibility and the Things a Man Did and Did Not Do. He would talk interminably overhead—pausing now and then to snip a dead flowerhead or pinch off a withering twig. And always during the walk Father would pick a single bloom, the most perfect he could find, and at the end of the walk he would take it in and present it to Mother with the same ritual phrase every Sunday morning, year after year: 'For you, my dear. Clifford and I have been talking.'

Father was inordinately proud of the two elms that grew at the entrance of the drive—they had been planted by his father before him and he often spoke to the boy about how he must care for them—as though in some way they were the living symbol of the House and the Family, and Life and Responsibility and the Things a Man Did and Did Not Do. The elms had begun to die in the year that he died...It was raining when he died—the Melbourne skies had wept for many days before he died. The boy had had to walk down the long stairs in the grey light of the afternoon and stand beside the open coffin and look at the terrible loneliness of the dead.

And then it was found that things were never quite the same after—Father's Responsibility had not carried on beyond his death. The elms died and the House died...

'That's a sunset,' said the Doc.

'What?' said Connell. 'Oh, yes.' The gravelled drive was gone and the white sand was heavy underfoot. The elms were dead and the jungle trees grew savagely.

Still, influence and tradition were enough to get some scraps of preferment. Outposts of the empire—life in the islands—heat, boredom and sterile lives—the wide-verandahed house—the natives in white—keeping up appearances and squabbling privately about money. He remembered the day he had come back from Moresby—a day earlier than he had told Phyllis...

'Where belongim missus?' he asked his headboy.

The boy, grinning, had held up the newborn kitten. 'Picaninny belongim cat come up along kai kai time.'

'To hell with the cat,' snarled Connell. 'Where belongim missus?'

'Catchim lik lik walk longa Boss Rannerson.'

Drinking—drinking alone and heavily—and then on the impulse striding out of the house—through the frangipanis and across the little board bridge across the creek and up towards the hill where Rannerson's house stood. Standing in the shadows watching the darkened house and listening to the smothered laughter and breathless murmuring and small cries. Life is savagery and despair.

'Look at that,' said the Doc. He held a scarlet branch of coral, curiously smooth and shaped like a stag's antler. Antlers, horns—the cuckold horns.

'What?' said Connell. 'Oh, yes.'

He could remember Rannerson coming to see him. Rannerson—big, brutally sensual and coarse with joviality.

'Look here, Connell, you're being a fool. What do you want to do: challenge me to a duel? Look, it's your own damn fault, coming home a day early—never come back home unexpected up here. It's the heat—they all get arse-end itchy—they go looking for it. On the other hand, you do the same thing—or wouldn't you care for me to mention Mae Thompson? You see, I'm not a gentleman, Connell—I'm not public school, or officer-and-gentleman or anything like you—I don't mind mentioning a woman's name in the mess. Look, come off it—we've all got to do something to fill in time here. I've had her, you've had her—and very nice too. Only we three know about it. Forget about it. Have a drink.'

Rannerson had called the boy himself and ordered the whisky. And Connell had drunk with him and hated himself. He and Phyllis had been together for a year after that, before the war separated them.

Lots of people try to run—from the past, the present or the future. What is the future? Thought rusts the brain and it sheds flakes of despair.

'As a matter of fact, I've got a flask of brandy,' said the Doc as they went back up the jungle path from the beach to the RAP. 'It's supply—I'll prescribe you a dose.'

'I'll take it, Mag,' said Connell. 'And after that—I will take a couple of your bloody pills, too.'

Pez and Janos and the Laird were lounging beside the muddy road at the bay when the General's jeep got bogged. She swung, roaring along the track, and came to rest belly-deep in mud. Pez and Janos and the Laird disappeared into the bushes instantly.

They saw the brass hats get out and walk around the stranded vehicle pontifically.

'Watch this,' whispered Pez. 'This'll be good.'

The General made a masterly military assessment of the problem. 'I think we'll have to dig it out,' he pronounced.

The Colonel pondered this gravely. 'What we need is a shovel,' he decided finally.

The Captain went and got the shovel—and gave it to the driver and he started to dig.

'That's the way of it,' rumbled the Laird. 'Right through the goddam army—everyone else makes the decisions, the poor bloody private does the job.'

Later, on their way back to the doover, they passed Connell on the track. He was looking particularly pleased with himself.

'I know what that means,' grunted the Laird. 'We'll be on the move again in a day or two. He's only happy when he's in a blue.'

We got ourselves a new lieutenant before we set out. Minnie, his name was—Minnie the Mouse. He'd been a Q bloke mostly and we'd left him at our base camp down the shore. But we'd lost so many officers they dragged him out and shot him up to us.

He was a funny little bloke—physically slight and extremely timid. He'd won his pips by passing brilliantly in theoretical work at an officers' school—if they'd left him at a desk job somewhere around Victoria Barracks he'd probably have given good and valuable service during the war.

It was his own fault, of course. He wanted to be a soldier—a fighting soldier—but he lacked all the equipment except that desire. It had got him as far as a commission in an infantry battalion and now it had finally got him a fighting platoon—but the job was not for him.

Minnie was an only child and he had a fond mother and father. Pez met his old man in town one leave...

He was strolling down Pitt Street and this old bloke in civvies pulled him up.

'I saw your colour patch,' he said. 'My son's in the same battalion as you—I thought you might know him—Sullivan's the name—Lieutenant Sullivan.'

Pez scratched his head—Sullivan—Sullivan—suddenly he remembered: 'Oh, God yes! I remember but mostly we call him...Oh, you know, we've got nicknames for all the officers.'

Near as dammit he'd said Minnie the Mouse. The old bloke probably wouldn't have liked that—he seemed proud as hell of Minnie being a Loot. A nice old bloke he was, too, but with those kind of soft rabbity eyes, just like Minnie.

The old bloke wanted to know what we called him and that had Pez worried for a bit.

'Munga,' he told him finally. 'That's what we call him—Munga—it's an old one from the Middle East.'

The old boy was pleased and proud.

'Oh yes, he was there, too,' he said. 'He was in the Middle East.'

Minnie had been a good son. He'd never whored around or got drunk and he'd lived all his life in timid frustration. He had paid court to a respectable young lady in a perfectly respectable fashion for years—the theatre on Thursdays, a dance on Saturdays, and a salad and cold meat dinner at her mother's place every Sunday. Her mother thought he was a nice boy and it was generally understood that they would marry when his bank balance and clerkly salary reached the proportions thought respectable.

The nearest Minnie got to respect as an officer was when the men said he 'wasn't a bad poor bastard'. The other skulls laughed at him behind his back—but managed to get him to do a good deal of their paperwork for them back in standing camp.

So this was our new officer. First Slapsy and then Minnie—we could certainly draw the crow.

They told us this might be the last show we would do before going home. We were to take over from the Second

Battalion for a while—then they would come through us and finish the stretch.

We were hearing rumours of another war, too. The second front had opened in Europe. We heard the news in whispers down the line—in occasional wireless news—in reports of men coming back from hospital.

While we marched along the long green shore men died in the steel ring of Cherbourg—the earth was stained more red at Arnhem—the Russian guns thundered as they rolled in the East. Something was happening north of us in the Pacific—there was a place called Iwo Jima.

So we went on—what was left of us. We struck good weather. The road was broad and hard. We were second platoon. The only Nips we saw were the dead ones that the sections in front left for us.

One day we halted near the body of a young Nip lying by the side of the track. It was smoko. Janos walked over and flopped down next to the body: 'Come on,' he invited Pez. 'It's all right, he doesn't stink. He's fresh.'

The Nip was only a lad—it's hard to tell with them, but he looked about eighteen. He had fallen forward on his face, his head was turned to the right and his legs sprawled. He had died swiftly, without struggle, and looked as though he had fallen in exhausted sleep. There were three bullet holes in his back, smudged black with blood around the edges—quite neat and seeming to bear no relationship to death. A trickle of blood had dried in the corner of his mouth. One hand was outflung and he still clutched a fresh bundle of plucked grasses—another bundle was tucked into his back pocket.

'Wonder why he was picking grass?' said Janos. 'He doesn't look as though he was hungry.'

The grasses were thick and juicy looking.

'I think it's that koyu the natives use,' said Pez. 'They say it's a good vegetable.'

'A man should have green vegetables,' said Janos. He took the grasses out of the hand of the dead man. He had to use force to bend the fingers back.

'You're not going to eat it, are you?' asked the Laird.

'Why not? If it won't kill him, it won't kill me.'

Janos made the stew that night and stirred the grass into it. None of the others except Pez would eat it with him. Pez didn't quite understand: 'What is this? A sacrificial supper?'

Janos just grinned.

They had pitched their doover facing the beach and Janos had gone down to the fires to make the stew while Pez dug the weapon pit.

The sun was slanting down when Janos got back. They sat on the edge of the weapon pit and ate the stew. It was good and hot, with flour stirred into it to thicken it. The dead Nip's grass tasted something like spinach, but faintly bitter. Neither said anything more about it.

It was stand to before they finished. First Janos crouched down in the pit and smoked, then Pez. They sat together, talking in low voices.

It was a safe billet and time to get a good rest. We were camped in a little belt of trees on the edge of the white sands. In front of us was the sea—behind us a broad dirt road. Other platoons were camped across the road, ahead and behind us.

Pez and Janos sat together on the edge of the weapon pit. The moon had risen before stand to ended and it was shining bright and silver on the sand and mottled on the road and left us in black shadows in the trees.

'It's been a long time, Pez,' said Janos. 'This is a hell of a business...'

'Yeah,' said Pez. 'It's been a long time—a lot of men...'

'I don't know what I go back to when it ends—if I'm left when it ends,' said Janos. 'Sometimes it bothers me.'

'Don't worry, boy,' said Pez. 'We're near enough to the end now—you're home and hosed—we'll drink a gallon of beer in Ma Maloney's yet.'

'When we first went away, home was close,' reflected Janos. 'You could remember it, and what you would do when you got back was clear.

'But it's been a long time now and things have changed. When you go back on leave the children you left behind—the kids next door—are men and women and you walk like a stranger in the street. People say hullo to you in the street and drink with you in the pubs and ask you how it was—but you don't really belong there—you're a wanderer, a blow-in, a ghost. They treat you with politeness, but not too lavishly. They spread themselves the first time you went away—they seem to resent it a bit now every time you come home again—they sent you away like a hero—they seem to expect that you should have done the decent thing and died like one—then they could feel satisfied they'd done right by you.

'If the war ended tomorrow, we'd be lost and lonely—we're lost and lonely now, so where's the beginning and the ending...?'

Pez made no answer—there was none to make. But it's a bad thing when a man starts talking about the future at times like this. In the rambling philosophy of a camp, that sort of thing is all right. But it's not a good thing to start thinking on those lines when you're on the track.

The whisper to stand down came floating through the trees.

'Come on, boy, let's sleep,' said Pez.

They were comfortable bunks in the clean sand that night—you could still feel the warmth of the sun on the earth through the blanket. Pez and Janos lay silent side by side under their tent flaps for a while. Then Janos said goodnight and rolled over. He was asleep in a few moments.

Pez lay awake and listened. There was a calm brooding silence on the beach. The hard, comforting feeling of his rifle lay beside him—the muzzle resting on the pack that made his pillow—a strange beloved to lie abed with. 'But I have known women who could be less cold, yet not so comforting,' he thought.

'Oh no, it couldn't be, Janos my brother—while we live we are not lost. All your courage and skill and wisdom cannot go for nothing. While we live we are not lost.'

Pez found himself thinking, for no reason, of the Deacon. He remembered one morning they had come up the track and on top of a sharp rise there was the body of a Nip ludicrously dead. His body made an arch, resting on head and feet, his naked backside poking up in the air.

We ran right into him as we topped the rise. The body was swollen and the skin had that tight, waxy look that they get. He was crawling.

The Deacon had paused in mock surprise—stepped back, sweeping his hat off, and bowed low to that backside: 'And good morning to you, sir,' said Deacon. 'The face is familiar but I'm afraid I can't quite place where I've met you.'

Why the hell should he remember Deacon...?

While we live we are not lost...

The Laird woke Pez for guard at two o'clock. He rolled out into the pit and sat there smoking a covered cigarette to wake himself properly.

Just before he was due to wake Janos, there were shots up the beach and a man came running down the sand. In the bright moonlight you could see he was a Nip. Pez fired, but it seemed he missed. Then an Owen opened up from further down. You could see the spurts of sand running across the beach towards him and then his body shuddered as the bullets struck him.

He started shrieking—a terrible, animal noise, and, turning, he rushed into the sea and was lost—though for long minutes afterwards you imagined you could hear the screams coming, pounded through the thunder of the surf.

Janos was behind Pez in the pit by now.

'Silly time for a bloke to go for a swim,' he said.

When we went forward that morning we ran into a Nip mountain gun. That was the finish of Minnie. It was the first time he had been under fire and he just ran around in circles. 'Like a chook with no head,' the Laird described it. He had no idea what to do. Whispering John and Harry Drew took charge. Minnie just crawled into a hole and stopped there.

A couple of days after that they sent Minnie back down the coast to the base camp. He was sent back as a neurosis case—an officer is entitled to get neurosis a damn sight quicker than a private.

It was that morning, too, that the Indians were shot. They'd escaped from the Nips and tried to get into our lines. They came down the track, waving bits of rag.

Young 'Squizzy' Taylor from Charley Company shot them down as they came. He was a bit nervous and Connell's orders were to take no prisoners. He didn't realise until he'd done it that they were our own men.

Two of them were dead when they got to them. The third they carried in and Doc Maguire worked over him all day—but he died.

The next day we took our objective—this was to be the end of the trail for us, they assured us.

We passed through a stretch of country that had been lived in once and was now overgrown. The roads were sunken but still definable. Everywhere was the ghostly smell and sign of the enemy—piles of rusting ammunition dumped along the side of the track—foxholes, weapon pits and dugouts burrowed in between the writhing octopus roots of the trees. For here, again, gnarled thick-limbed nightmare trees grew twisted into violent still life. Dozens of burned and rusting trucks were entangled in the jungle growth at the side of the roads—most of them had the skeleton of the driver underneath and the steel cabins were punched full of holes where the planes had strafed them.

At intervals were stacks of boxes with Japanese lettering burned on the sides. The boxes had rotted in the rain and burst with the weight of their contents—ammunition and equipment, but never food or clothing.

Our objective was a clearing a little inland. There was nothing to it. We went carefully along the track and reached the clearing without any trouble. There was a native hut in the centre. We riddled it from the edge of the clearing and then ran up to it.

Old Whispering John it was that kicked open the door. Janos and Pez and the Laird went on to clear the other side. Young Sunny covered old John. The rest of the platoon took ground.

Old John told the story later. He leaned his chin affectionately on Janos' shoulder and sniggered confidentially: 'There's this Nip there,' he whispered. 'He's lying on the bed and when I kick the door in he staggers to his feet. So I let him have a burst in the guts.' He sniggered. 'He walks round the room for a while holding his guts—and then he goes and lies on the bed.'

'Maybe he was tired!' snarled Janos—twisting his head to avoid old John's foul breath.

The war in Europe ended.

Young Sunny came running along the track: 'They've tossed it in—the Huns have tossed it in!' he yelled.

'Take it easy,' growled the Laird.

No one danced on the long green shore because the war in Europe had ended. A big shoal of fish had come in near the beach that morning—in close enough for our grenades. We had fresh fish for breakfast and that was more important just for the moment.

It was something to talk about, sure. But what the hell! Europe was a long way from us—our war was still going—it would take time to swing armies and air force men from Europe to the Pacific—our job was still to do, and time was the deadly factor.

It is a simple equation—the old blokes are the most worried—matter-of-factly worried. A soldier may have a thousand lives—no more. You can stand up just so many times and after that, no more. The longer you go, the higher the odds pile up. These old blokes have bowed to death so often—they know their time is running out.

It was that day, too, that Pez went back to hospital. He had been up all night with vomiting and diarrhoea. He was a pale shivering shell in the morning.

'You've got the wog all right, boy,' said Janos.

'Feels like it,' chattered Pez. His eyes were swimming, his skin burning, he was deadly cold inside.

Janos carried his pack for him down to the RAP.

'Don't worry about it, boy,' he said. 'This looks like the end of it. They reckon we're finished now. The Second's taken over and our next trip will be home. If we get home, the way things are shaping, we'll never go away again—she'll be all over before that.'

Doc Maguire took a look at Pez.

'Looks like a touch of the wog,' he said cheerfully.

'But even if it's not we'll send you back for a bit of rest—fatten you up a bit. Have you been eating all right?'

'Oh, not badly, on and off, Doc,' shivered Pez.

'Thought so,' said the Doc. 'A bit of starvation is what's wrong with you.'

'I'll make sure they send your letters back,' said Janos. 'Look after yourself, boy.'

Pez lay down on a stretcher with a couple of blankets over him while he waited for the ambulance. He could keep nothing in his stomach. They gave him a cup of tea—he brought it up. They gave him a dose of quinine—it came up immediately and the bitter sting of it remained at the back of his nose.

All the world is dazed and pitched off-key. The body loses substance.

There is only one other patient in the three-tonner ambulance truck with him—a young lad from the Second Battalion with a leg wound. He grunts a little as the truck bumps and sways down the road. His eyes are a little hysterical—too much white showing in them—and his voice rambles...

'I cut their throats,' he is saying. 'We never took any prisoners in our mob—I cut their throats—even the dead ones. After it's finished I go around and cut their throats—even the dead ones.'

He falls silent and groans between his teeth as the truck grinds and bumps down in a rough pinch.

'My brother was in Malaya,' he says. 'They killed my brother in Malaya—some blokes who were with him told me—they cut his throat like a pig...'

They waited half an hour at the ambulance station at the 'drome for the plane to come in. There are other cases there—stretcher cases mostly that have been carried down from the hills.

From where Pez sits he can see across into the hospital itself—a casualty clearing station. The sides of one of the tents is drawn back for the light. Three or four white robed figures move around the table, bending over it. Red flesh is showing on the naked figure strapped to the table.

The plane comes.

On the trip down he crouches near a window and with hot, heavy eyes stares at the meaningless drift of jungle and shore that flows beneath him—the long green shore that so painfully and darkly they had fought and marched along. All the weary weeks it had taken them and now it passes in a brief twenty minutes.

The first thing you feel when you get into hospital is a sense of your own dirtiness—the grime that has been under your fingernails unnoticed for months suddenly seems gritty and itchy on the tips of your fingers.

There is no glory in the world like a hot shower—you come out purged and clean—your whole body is light as in a dream. It must be a thousand years since you were clean before.

There is a rare pleasure in the lightness and cleanliness of unaccustomed pyjamas and your feet are shod with air in slippers after the heavy jungle boots.

For the first week, Pez slept, mostly. Sleeping for a couple of hours and waking briefly to drift back again. It is an unreal world of polite voices and soups and sweets with meals and lights at night and music from the loudspeaker beating softly through the long palm-leafed ward. This is peace and rest—but somehow it is further away from home and reality than the weapon pit is. Here are books and morning tea with biscuits and women—brisk and professionally tender—so neatly starched in khaki, so sweet-smelling, so soft of face—how coolly warm their fingers are on your brow—but we are further from home, this is peaceful desolation.

Harry Drew and Regan visit Pez. They are on their way back to the battalion. He hears news of others. Some are dead, some have gone home, some are in hospital still, some have gone back up the track.

At the end of the first week they put a bloke with pleurisy into the end bed next to Pez. He was dying. For three days they fought for him. There was always a nurse by his side. Bottles of plasma and serum and glucose were suspended over his bed, the long red tubes snaking down. The life-liquids dripped into his veins hour after hour. The nurses sat by him and smoothed his brow and tried to calm him when he raved and brushed moist cotton wool on his parched lips when he begged and groaned for water.

The third night he called out a lot and the doctors came many times. When Pez woke in the morning the bed was empty and the bottles had been taken down. The little nurse called Bunty was sniffling and red-eyed as she remade the bed. She had been with him at the last. It must be hard to fight so long and passionately and skilfully and then have them die under your hands.

*

When Pez gets up and about again he makes way a bit with Bunty. They really got acquainted one day when he strolled into the storeroom out the back of the ward to get a fresh towel.

The linen cabinet was a dark little cubicle and Pez, groping his way in blindly from bright sunshine outside, ran bang into Bunty who was inside the cubicle doing a quick change act.

'Hell! I'm sorry,' said Pez, retreating hastily from that disturbing soft nakedness.

He leaned against the wall outside the cubicle and lifted his eyes ostentatiously to heaven: 'Why don't you hang out a sign—lady undressing?'

'What the devil are you doing here, anyway?' asked Bunty, amused. 'You're not supposed to be here.'

'I was after a clean towel,' confessed Pez. 'I missed out on the issue.'

A suggestively naked arm came out of the cubicle with a laundered towel: 'If a towel's all you're after, that's a change. Usually you blokes are after something else once you get on your feet.'

'Oh, I'm adaptable,' said Pez. 'I can turn my hand to practically anything.'

Bunty came out of the darkness, buttoning her jacket: 'In that case,' she said evilly, 'and on account of the embarrassment you've caused me, you can give me a hand to do some ironing.'

So Pez helped Bunty do the ironing and spent a lot of time talking to her casually and smoking her cigarettes as he worked. It was a very casual and comradely affair.

Once she did suggest that if he could dig up a bottle of whisky somewhere she was very partial to whisky and knew a very comfortable and private sandhill—but Pez couldn't lay hands on a bottle of whisky.

When he was leaving she kissed him in a friendly fashion and they made a date for a pub crawl in Sydney after the war.

The ward next door was the troppo ward. It was closed in with heavy cyclone wire and guarded by provosts. Odd cries and yells came from it at times.

There was one bloke Pez could see and hear through the wire. He was a big bloke. His left arm was smashed and in plaster.

He would stand for hours looking out through the wire—the fingers of his good hand hanging onto the wire above his head, his smashed hand held against his stomach, his face pressed against the mesh.

For a long time he would stand quietly. Then suddenly he would open his mouth wide and give vent to a long animal scream that went on and on—at the same time seeming quite detached from him. His calmly insane face was visible through the wire, the mouth wide open, and those agonised shrieks seemed to be coming from some other being locked inside him.

He escaped one day.

The first Pez knew was when he saw him running. He came with a peculiar loping run, his smashed hand, weighted with the plaster, swinging pendulum-like. He was crowing in a thin wailing voice as he ran and chuckling with childish triumph.

He came running into the ward and went straight to the little bald-headed bloke in the bed opposite Pez. He lay down on the bed, snuggled down.

'I got away from them, Eddie,' he chuckled with childish triumph. 'Look, see!' He was showing his dead meat tickets with a furtive, confidential air. 'Look, Eddie—you know me—I'm a Protestant—they're all Hindus in there—I'm a Protestant and they're trying to make me a Hindu—but I got away—' he shivered again with delighted childish laughter.

'Sure, sure, she'll be right, Happy,' said Eddie. 'You'll be all right here.'

Half a dozen provosts came running into the ward. Big, beefy blokes, panting from the run. They crowded round the bed but none of them seemed to be anxious to be first.

The man with the smashed arm cowered back on the bed, snarling. When they tried to grab him he kicked at them and beat at them with his plaster arm. He was shrieking incoherent filth at them, the teeth and red gums showing in his savage mouth.

Eddie had his arms around him.

'Get away from him! Get away!' Eddie was pleading. 'Leave him alone! He'll smash his arm again—he's smashed it three times already.'

There was an angry growl from the rest of the ward, a swift gathering anger: 'Provost! Provost! Let him alone!'

The little dark-eyed Sister was in the middle of the provosts suddenly, ordering them back: 'Get outside, boys,' she said. 'I'll handle this.'

'He's dangerous, Sister,' said one provost. 'He tried to use a knife.'

'Get outside,' she said.

The bloke with the smashed arm was still snarling—watching the provosts. They withdrew to the doorway.

The dark-eyed Sister walked calmly up to the bed and stood close to him. Everyone in the long ward held their breath. Slowly her hand went out and rested lightly on his forehead.

'Are you all right, lad?' she asked.

He looked at her a long moment—gradually the snarl faded, the distorted face relaxed. He looked at her with utter weariness—the tormented eyes finding rest in the cool and unpitying warmth of her.

'Yes, Sister, I'm all right—only make them go away—see, I'm a Protestant—see, I can show you my meat tickets—they're all Hindus—make them go away, Sister.'

She ordered the provosts away. They go reluctantly. She stayed quietly talking to him. 'How do you feel?' she asked.

'All right, Sister—I'm all right—just my head aches.'

She soothed his brow—oh, those hands had the sweetness of a benediction and like cool water soothed our fevers.

'I just want to stay here with my mates, Sister—I know they want to put me on a plane tonight—I'll go on the plane, Sister, but I just want to stop here with my mate until then—this is my mate, Eddie—I just want to stay here with him and sleep.'

The little bald-headed bloke, Eddie, had him in his arms, nursing him.

'He'll be all right, Sister,' said Eddie. 'I'll look after him—he'll be all right until the plane.'

The Sister asked will she bring another bed in for him, to put alongside Eddie's bed, but Eddie said no, he's comfortable—he'll look after him.

The little bald-headed bloke sat there holding the big bloke in his arms all the afternoon. Sometimes the big bloke slept, other times he talked in a swift confidential little whisper and showed Eddie his meat tickets.

He was calm in the evening but the provosts came in again and he kicked and screamed when he saw one of them with the morphia shining in his hand.

The dark-eyed little Sister came in again.

The provosts left him and the big bloke finally went quietly with Eddie.

'I know they want me on the plane,' he said. 'I'll go on the plane—just so long as they keep away from me.'

In the small bay of the island where the convalescent camp was, a rough wooden jetty jutted out from the shrill white sand. Draped over the rail of the jetty was a long, lean American. He stared morosely down into the clear water and, with backwoods accuracy, spat from time to time at the coral-coloured fish that drifted up to the surface and flicked away.

Another American came down onto the beach. 'Hey, Hank!' he yelled through cupped hands. 'The Cap'n warnts you!'

The tall, morose citizen spat into the water. 'Go tell the Cap'n,' he yelled back, 'tuh take a flyin' fark at a gallopin' goose—I ain't a'comin'!'

This pleasantry so intrigued Pez that he sought further acquaintance: 'What's the matter, Yank?' he asked. 'You sound browned-off.'

'Man,' said the American, 'I been goosed and gart at—this here base ain't nothin' from beginnin' tuh end but hart cark!'

'What?' queried Pez.

'Cark!' said the American. 'C-O-C-K—cark!'

'Don't you think the Captain might be disturbed that you won't join him?' asked Pez.

The American spat again. 'He's a cark sarker from Fifth Avenoo—I know him frum way back—when I tell him I ain't a'comin' he knows I ain't a'comin'.'

'You've got your army organised properly,' admired Pez.

'We gart organisation,' said the American. 'We gart organisation like I gart a hole in the head—it takes a whole garddamn army to organise me so I set on my ass arn this gard forsaken pimple arn the ass end uv the world, while I gart a redhead waitin' for me back at Kings Crarss...man, she's hart and she's strong for me! She's gart legs like Grable and tits like you never saw in a dream. And I set here on my ass on a pimple on the ass end uv the world—and the Cap'n warnts to see me!'

'I got a girl up near the Cross myself,' said Pez. 'It's all right—she's not a redhead.' He pulled his wallet out and opened it at the photo of Helen.

'Say, she's sharp,' admired the American. 'She's gart class.'

He dug out his own wallet. 'No, nart that one—that's muh wife. This other one—that's muh Bella.'

'I see what you mean,' admired Pez.

'Oh man, she was hart,' mourned the American, 'and strong for me. Incidentally, my name's Hank.'

'Mine's Pez.'

'Look, I gart a case uv canned beer—tastes like parrot's piss—would you care to join me?'

'Never knocked one back yet,' said Pez.

'Well, carm on—we'll go arp round the back way—I wouldn't drink with any uv the cark sarkers here—they all like to play soldiers—so long as the garddamned war ain't too close, they like it fine.'

'Say, Pez,' said Hank, a couple of nights later. Whut's this garddamned swy—this two-arp you basstuds play?'

'Come and I'll show you,' offered Pez. As they struck off across the island to the swy school, he instructed Hank. 'Now, you've seen the game, haven't you?'

'Yes, uh've seen it,' admitted Hank, 'but I never gart close enough to it—looks like all cark to me.'

'Well, you see, you've got a ring—you've got a boxer, he holds the stake money—you've got a ringie, he hands the kip on and calls the bets—a spinner comes in with two pennies on the kip...'

'Whart's the garddamned kip?'

'A little piece of board that you rest the pennies on when you toss them. Then when the guts is set and you're set on the side...'

'Whart's this garddamned guts and side?'

'Well, the guts is the centre—the stake your spinner is spinning for. That's got to be set first and then any bets on the side are set. The spinner's usually for heads—if you're a tail better you set the centre or bet against another headie on the side. Then the ringie calls, "Set in the guts, all set on the side—come in spinner," and up go the pennies. You can bar them if they float or if you don't think it's a fair go—but you've got to bar them in the air. Down they come and the ringie calls the result—heads or tails—or ones, no result. If you're spinning for a head and you do them, she rides and you double up to the third, then the boxer takes his drag. On the fourth you can drag some yourself—but if you let her ride she doubles every time. If you can do a dozen in a big school you got a fortune.'

'Whart happens if you tail 'em?'

'You pass the kip—you've had it.'

The school was in some dead ground over at the back of the island. The ring was a canvas square lit with globes powered from truck batteries. There were thirty or forty at the game and the ringie, a short, villainous-looking character, was skipping around the canvas in his stockinged feet and bellowing hoarsely: 'Come on! We want another quid in the guts to see him go—just one more fiddly from you tailies—come on, he's done 'em five—I want a tailie for a quid to see him go!'

'Why, I guess I'll accommodate you for that,' said Hank.

The ringie looked up at the accent as though his favourite and long-lost brother had just walked in. He took Hank's pound and tossed it to the boxer, who was crouched on a kerosene case at the edge of the ring, with the centre money laid out in little heaps of individual bets in front of him. The boxer covered Hank's pound and the ringie shouted with renewed enthusiasm, 'Come on, get set on the side—any more bets on the side—he's done five already—any money for a head, any money for a tail. Right! Set in the centre, set on the side—it's a fair go—come in spinner!'

The ringie eased to the side of the ring and muttered to the boxer out of the corner of his mouth, 'Did you cop the septic tank just walked in? We might make wages yet tonight.'

The spinner weighed the pennies carefully on the kip and looked up to measure his objective or seek help from God...

'Ring out!' bellowed the ringie hoarsely. 'Ring out, he's a high spinner.'

'Whart the garddamned hell does he warnt now?' demanded Hank.

'Give him room, he throws them high,' said Pez.

The spinner tossed the pennies up high and back over his head, giving a little hop for luck as he did so. The coins rang together in the air and the ringie shouted with unconvincing playfulness: 'Jingles for joy! Ring back—I'll call them!' The coins slapped and rolled on the canvas—heads craned—the Lady glared up in two places. 'He's micked 'em,' announced the ringie morosely. 'Pay the tails—and what about a bit of a sling from you headies!'

'Man,' said Hank as he got his two pounds back. 'This here's a game! I can work out a system.'

A quarter of an hour later, and twenty pounds lighter, he and Pez trudged back across the island. 'Jesse James,' said Hank, 'Dillinger, Capone—we've had them back in the States—but never nothin' like that game.'

Hank poked his head into the tent as Pez was packing to go back to the mainland. 'Here, Pez,' he said, 'I gart you two cartons uv cigarettes. Couldn't get you any garddarmned Luckies—these here are made out uv shag shit—but they burn.'

Pez dragged a Nip flag out of his pack. 'I got you the flag, Hank. She's genu-wine—my mate finished making her this morning. I shot the holes in it myself and when the tomato sauce dries you won't be able to tell it from blood.'

'Thanks Pez,' said Hank.

'And apart from that, I got you a story to go with it,' said Pez. He struck a pose. 'This here flag, my friends, was captured in the bloody fighting before we took the Nip headquarters at Booma Ridge. Defended it was by a company of Nip Royal Marines—all six feet high and fighting fools who had sworn a Shinto, Banzai, Kamikaze oath that the flag would not fall into the hands of the enemy while one of them remained alive.'

With an expression of awe, Hank sat down on the bed.

'For two days and two nights we were locked in mortal combat on that hill, friends—it was tough, mighty tough—until the only man of the Nip guard remaining alive was Captain Sake Sake. He draped the flag around his body, drew his sword and charged down the hill, till he fell in the face of withering fire. Here are the holes, you see, my friends—these same holes are where the bullets pierced the flag and struck mortally into the body of Major Sake Sake.'

'He gart quick promotion,' said Hank.

'And these same ominous stains, friends, are where his lifeblood flowed as he died to honour his oath!'

'Jee-sus Christ!' said Hank reverently. 'That's hart, man. That sure is the hartest kind uv cark!'

'I'd have got his sword for you too,' apologised Pez, 'but my mate over at workshops hasn't quite finished making it. She'll be right, though—made out of the best quality jeep spring and with Colonel Sake Sake's family history tastefully engraved on the blade—gen-u-wine Samurai. He'll bring it over the day after tomorrow.'

'That'll be fine, Pez,' said Hank. 'I'll trade it to some uv these new cark sarkers that are comin' out. They admire to get somethin' with bullet holes and blood so they can tell the folks back home how they waded knee deep in it—and just what fightin'est sons uv bitches they really are. I'll sock 'em plenty.'

They walked to the barge together.

'Say, Pez,' said Hank. 'If you happen to be in Noo Yark after the war, remember two thousan' one hunnerd and thirty-five on Thirty-Fifth Street. You'll find it easy—anyone'll tell you.'

'Yeah,' said Pez. 'Well, don't forget what I told you: the back bar at the Imperial at the Cross, any time after five. Ask Eileen.'

As the barge drew out from the jetty, Hank leaned over the rail, 'See you after the war, man. Don't forget.' He was calling across the water: 'Two thousan' one hunnerd and thirty-five on Thirty-Fifth Street—Noo Yark.' A thought struck him, he bellowed: 'City!'

There were only a handful of men at the base camp, but rations were still light on and the main source of supply was still the Yank rubbish dumps.

Pez struck the Log at the camp and they met the blokes left behind when we went up the long green shore, and caught up on all the gossip. Sergeant Buney, the Vickers sergeant, who had developed bad feet mysteriously just before we moved, had been making a pretty penny selling stuff belonging to blokes who had been killed—stuff left behind in their kitbags in the battalion store. There were a few mutterings among the boys about it, but nothing was ever done about him—no complaint was made. The dead can't complain.

On their way down to the mess, Minnie the Mouse stuck his head out of a tent. He seemed surprised and grateful when Pez hailed him.

'Coming down to eat?' asked Pez.

'No, thanks,' said Minnie. He seemed shy of something. 'No—as a matter of fact I'm writing a letter.'

Pez glanced into the tent. There was a small deal table set for the light, a writing pad, pen and ink, and an inch-thick pile of what looked like manuscript. 'Looks like some letter,' Pez said. 'You nearly finished it?'

'Well, no,' said Minnie. He seemed a bit embarrassed, but pleased to talk to someone. 'As a matter of fact, it's a very difficult letter to write.'

It appears Minnie had been hanging around the base camp for some time. They were going to board him south with some honourable and comfortable neurosis of the type reserved for officers. Then he got a letter from his girl—the one he'd wooed respectably for going on nine years.

It wasn't a very long letter. In fact, pretty near everyone around the base knew it by heart. It was just two lines, announcing that Dorothy was going to marry a British commando named Bruce. It was signed, with rather unhappy formality, 'Yours faithfully'.

A couple of nights after he received the letter, Minnie attended the open-air picture show down at the hospital area. While a faithless lady on the screen was entertaining her lover, he rose babbling incoherently and emptied his revolver into the screen.

They took his revolver off him, but decided later that he was not really dangerous and let him go back to the unit base camp to wait for a plane south.

Now he sat in his tent all day and wrote. He wouldn't attend the normal mess parade, but it was suspected that he used to sneak down to the kitchen at night and get tinned stuff.

All day long he would sit writing. There was a great wad of manuscript when Pez last saw it. He asked Minnie if he'd like it posted, but Minnie said it wasn't finished yet.

Pez's mail finally caught up with him. There were half-a-dozen letters from Helen—the last ones written after the war in Europe ended. 'Come home,' she said. 'Be careful and come home to me.'

He felt warm and benevolent on the strength of it and went to talk to Minnie for a while to try and cheer him up. Then later he got to thinking about it.

'Come home,' she said. Sure, she said that—but he had to go home to the problem—that still stood—there were still three where only two could go.

A woman might write a thing like that—and mean it for the moment—but when he did get home...

The last night at the camp, Pez got very drunk on home-distilled gin and sat very late in his tent writing to Helen.

*My Darling, My Dearest, My Honey,*

*I'm on my way back to the unit after Con Camp. Your letters caught up with me today. I've read them all through many times and I feel there's something tremendously important I've got to say. The only trouble is, I don't know what it is—I've sat here for hours trying to think what it is I want to say.*

*Possibly this is complicated by the fact that I'm drunk on gin made fresh this afternoon by Bill Abdou (you remember him) from Workshops. In fact, I am as drunk as*

*Chloe—full as a bull—or a boot, or a goog—molo—pissed as a newt or (if you prefer it) to the eyebrows.*

*Or maybe it's the thought—the impossible, fantastic thought that the war might some time, soon now, be over. What that will mean to us, I don't know.*

*I suppose that is what troubles me, really—I am looking for a meaning. That's it—the wonder of the world. The meaning of living—the meaning of death—the meaning of love. Is living being alive and death ceasing to be alive and loving tumbling on a bed? I ask this question without notice of the Honourable Minister for Human Affairs.*

*Helen, my dearest, I am drunk and I love you. I am coming back—and to you. I don't care what arguments there are against it—I am coming back to take you. I am drunk and I love you. I love you even more, sober, but not so poetical. Goodnight my love, my dearest. You are the Song of Songs, which is Solomon's, and if your belly is not quite a heap of wheat set about with lilies, it will do until a heap of wheat set about with lilies comes along.*

*I am drunk and biblical and bedevilled and damned... and I want a meaning. I look up at the sky and wonder—and I look down at the earth and wonder—and I dream on you and wonder. The wonder of the world.*

*I am drunk—and Christ I miss you and I need you.*

The word came suddenly. Everyone except base personnel to move that evening.

'I don't like the look of this, Pez,' grumbled the Log. 'Why do they want everyone in such a damn hurry?'

They tumbled onto a barge just before dark and after a beaten-iron voyage, the monstrous, clanging, stinking creature flopped its jaw up on the sand next morning and they stumbled from its crowded throat.

The doover tents were knocked down in the battalion area and the packs loaded for the track.

Janos grinned when he saw Pez slogging up the hill. 'How are you, boy? Ready for the track? The bastards have pulled us in again.'

It seemed the Second had struck a bit of trouble down the shore and we were to cut inland and come in on the Nips' flank.

It was a hell of a thing to have to do. To start over again when we thought we were finished—when we thought the war might have ended for us.

A couple of the older blokes are left behind—ones who have been in it since practically the first day. The Log is one and the Laird another. But old Whispering John comes. 'The old soldier'll see it through,' he cackles.

The Log and the Laird stand by the side of the track and wave to us as we go—they look kind of naked and lonely standing there in just shirts and slacks while we slog down the track armoured in webbing equipment and packs.

Harry Drew had been supposed to stay. Regan had said goodbye to him: 'You're not coming, Harry, I'll see you when she's all over.'

But Harry came with us.

Young Regan walked behind him as he led us down the track.

# 7

We struck into the hills—savage tracks that scrambled up and slithered down. It is the old story—patrolling, probing, killing. We are all apprehensive about it, I think—we are all afraid of it this time—we had been so near the end.

There are frequent clashes with Connell over the native boys who come with us into the hills. We talk to them and give them an occasional cigarette, they're good boys—but Connell objects.

'You don't understand them,' he says, 'they're just like children. Planters have got to work these boys again after the war's finished and you're ruining them.'

'Yeah, we're ruining them,' snarls Harry Drew later. 'They'll want an extra bob a day after the war—we're ruining them—cutting down the profits.'

There was that day in the hills that Harry Drew came

up laughing like hell. He'd just heard the best story of the year—Watson, that Angau bloke had told him.

It seemed this happened before the First World War. One of the mission stations along the coast had a fine coconut plantation. The missionaries had done a splendid job of the joss and had so impressed the natives with their hellfire that they one and all became devout Christians.

The missionaries had been very careful to explain to the converted heathen that they were working for the Lord now—everything belonged to the Big Pfella Jesus and the copra had to be carefully gathered and shipped away to the same Big Pfella Jesus.

Well, one time when the missionaries were away on tour, leaving the mission to their head boy, a trader calls in and tries to buy some copra. But the head and all the other boys explain to him that they can't sell any copra, that it all belongs to the Big Pfella Jesus, and they bring out little coloured Sunday School cards of Jesus to show just who the big boss is.

Well, the trader, who is a man of imagination, goes back to his schooner and drinks a square bottle of gin with his raffish mate and has a long think. As a result of this he goes for a little trip around the islands, waiting for his beard to grow nice and long. Then he comes back and waits until he gets word that the missionaries are away on tour again.

He dresses himself and his mate in robes of blasphemous white and, with a bunch of black heathens dancing and waving palm leaves before him, he strides into the mission yard, raises his hand and declares in a voice of the mountains, 'I am Big Pfella Jesus and I have come for my copra!'

And the faithful mission boys worked like slaves to get the copra onto the boat for him. When it was all loaded, the trader called them all together and prayed over them fervently and blasphemously in pidgin: "You pfella boys, good boys—supposim you catchim longa me Heaven—plenty kai kai, number one—plenty pom pom, number one..." and he went around as they knelt in the dust and laid a godless paw devoutly on each woolly head and sprinkled his own special brand of holy water from a gin bottle with the label carefully washed off. Then he presents the head boy with the bottle and the little bit of holy water left in it for his own use and tells him he's a number one good boy. Back he goes to his ship, with his own heathen crew dancing and waving palm leaves before him, and away he sails.

We asked Tamal, the big police boy, what he thought of the missionaries.

Tamal grinned sourly: 'Too much Jesus, not enough kai kai,' he declared.

So we gave him a tin of bully.

Janos kills two more Nips as forward scout, but when Connell passes on the track Janos doesn't move to add up the score for him.

It was the morning after we took the last village on the western ridge that the Indian came in.

A youngish man, he was, but he looked ancient and bone-thin with the dirty-grey pallor of starvation shining through the Punjab copper of his skin. He had crouched all night in the rain outside the sentry lines and came in half an hour after dawn, waving a piece of cloth and crying:

'Master! Master! Don't shoot—Indian! Indian!'

He kept up his shrill, quavering cry until he was well inside the perimeter. Then, when he saw he was safe, he suddenly stopped and was shaken with a fierce, cold fit of shivering.

'Tired—tired—hungry,' he told Pez and Janos who were taking him back to Company headquarters.

He tried to tell them of the years of starvation and death that had passed since his capture and of the great fear that possessed him when he walked towards the sentry crying shrilly: 'Don't shoot! Don't shoot!' The Nips had told them that the Australians would shoot on sight and there had been rumours about the other Indians who tried to give themselves up down the shore and had been shot waving the white flag.

He had escaped the previous day and crept in terror through the bush to the Australian lines. In the afternoon, at a hidden waterhole, he had carefully washed the piece of cloth he had used as a white flag. As he waited, an Australian patrol had drifted swiftly and silently along the ridge above him. He had wanted to call out to them, but he had been afraid.

Then, as it grew dark, he had crawled as close as he dared to the Australian perimeter and crouched there all night. In the morning he had walked in—expecting every minute to feel the numbing sting of bullets punching into his flesh—with the great agony of freedom so near, swelling in his breast—and then the terrible flood of weakness and fierce shuddering that took him when he realised he was free, he was safe...

He tried to tell them all about it, but all he could do was to look at Pez and Janos with a pathetic grin, gesturing round the camp and then to himself and chanting softly: 'Good—good—good.'

Pez reported him in to headquarters.

'Bloke here by the name of Ranjit,' he said. 'Been ack-willie for three years—reporting back for duty.'

Captain Baird talked to Ranjit, then told him to wait while he contacted Battalion, back down the track.

'What about giving him a feed, Cap?' said Janos. 'Looks as though tucker's been a bit light on for him.'

'Sure,' said Baird, 'take him over to your kitchen.'

So Pez and Janos took him over to the kitchen and the mob gathered round to try and talk to Ranjit. They gathered he had been taken in Singapore and had been a slave of the Nips ever since. Of the company of ninety of his countrymen that they had brought to New Guinea with him, only fifteen were now left alive.

You could almost see the strength and life flowing back into his body and his eyes as he tried to tell them where the Nips were and how strong they were and what had happened to him.

And the mob grinned with delight as they watched him put away the biggest issue of bully beef stew that any one man ever put away. 'Good on you, mate,' they said, and grinned at him. He grinned back as he ate and smoked the cigarettes they rolled for him.

As he passed through the Company on his way back down the track to Battalion, Ranjit wore a huge grin and greeted every single person he passed with a salute and a bow. The privates grinned at him with delight and returned his salute and said, 'Good on you, mate!' but some of the officers were uncomfortable and seemed uncertain whether to return his salute or smile benignly.

'Good morning, sah—good morning, sah,' said Ranjit, on his triumphal way. He got well to the top of the first hill then collapsed quite suddenly.

Old Doc Barnes, the medical orderly from Don Company, cursed the bloody fools who had let him stuff so much bully beef into himself and called for the stretcher bearers.

So Ranjit was carried back in triumph—suffering from malnutrition and over-eating.

It was about this time we found what had apparently been a big Nip base camp—crumbling buildings and piles of incense and rotting junk. We salvaged some postcards out of the mess—miracles of exquisite fragility in design.

Pez and Janos found the door to the big cave-like room dug out at the back of the store room. Pez kicked the rotting door away and Janos twisted a bunch of dried cane into a torch and lit it. By the flaring, smoky light they could see that the room was crammed with shelves all filled with small metal containers, each bearing numbers and symbols. Pez took one down and opened it. Inside was a handful of ashes.

'Ashes,' said Janos. 'Ashes of the dead. They're names

and numbers on those boxes. Christ, there are thousands of them. This was an army.'

In the smoky red flare of the cane torch, thousands of metal containers crouched on the shelves of that cave-like room, each bearing a name and a number, each containing its handful of ashes.

This was an army.

The fantastic news came through the day before we attacked the final hill.

We got it from the sig wires, up from the beach—it sounded like: 'They dropped one bomb and a city was destroyed.' The sig wires kept repeating something about an atomic bomb—atomic bomb. As we were waiting to go down the valley to that hill, everyone was talking about it.

'It sounds fantastic,' said Harry Drew, 'but these are days when fantastic things happen—they've been splitting the atom for years, of course...'

'Drop another one,' said Pez. 'Drop a dozen and finish this bloody business quick.'

'I don't know,' said Harry Drew. 'I don't know if it's the sort of thing that should be used—a whole city—women and children.'

'Is one big bomb any different to ten thousand small ones?' demanded Pez. 'They kill women and children just the same.'

'It sounds horrible,' said Janos. 'It sounds frightening.'

'Yes,' agreed Pez, after a pause. 'It's frightening—but it might save a lot more lives in the long run.'

*

‘B’ Company were ahead of us and we had to pass through them. Their headquarters were set on a little flat knoll at the junction of three tracks. The Sally tent was set up on the highway and the coffee urns were out and smoking. We stopped for coffee and biscuits and the talk was all of an atom bomb—‘One bomb, one city!’ They were incredulous, and yet it seemed right.

There was a small graveyard to the right of the track, opposite the Sally tent. There were three crosses and one open pit. As we finished our coffee, and filed away from the tent we could see the Don Company boys bringing the body up from down the valley.

It was a bad track to the left—knee-deep in black, slimy mud. They had the corpse, wrapped in a grey blanket, lashed to a litter and they had tied themselves to it with ropes.

The leader would give a shout and they would all fling themselves against the ropes, grunting and plunging against the thick, clinging mud and dragging the corpse and the four men who were carrying and steadying the litter, half a dozen wild staggering yards at a time—until they stopped exhausted and bogged down. All of them—the men on the ropes and the carriers and the corpse on the blanket—were plastered from head to foot in stinking black mud.

It was young Jimmy Travers—that little fair-haired bloke who came out from doing three months in Groverley only a week before we sailed.

We are pinned down.

Right at the foot of the track that clambers crazily up the hillside to the ridge we must win, we are pinned down under fire from the Nip weapon pits that are dotted left to right up the slope—deadly pockmarks on each side of the track.

We are bound in terror to the earth under their fire. We will never rise.

But Janos is calling for grenades—and suddenly, incredibly, he is standing—black hail is falling and he is standing! And, incredibly, we are standing, too—and he is screaming: 'Come on, you bastards! Do you want to live forever?'

We are running—we are charging—we are shouting! We are gods and madmen! Janos standing and his screaming of that terrible, fatal cry of battle that has been flung down the centuries—it drags us from the earth and storms us—laughing, yelling, screaming, stabbing, snarling, firing—it hurls us up the hill.

We win the ridge. The enemy is dead behind us, but ahead he still lives. Again we are driven to the earth, and this time we cannot rise. We are bound naked to the earth. Darkness falls, but still we cannot move. We must lie till dawn, clasping the earth in the agony of fear. Until dawn, when our comrades can attack on that other hill.

It had been dark and filled with death a long, long time. The Nips had been tossing grenades—blast grenades—must have been all they had. There was no shrap, but the concussion beat like a mighty hammer blow on the earth, which shuddered and trembled in your embrace—it smacked like a fist at the nape of your neck.

Pez could hear Janos' voice—a long way away, it seemed—small and frightened, whispering: 'Pez...Pez... Where are you...? Pez... Pez...'

Pez dragged himself inches into the darkness towards a vague shape that whispered.

'Here, boy, what's wrong?'

Janos wriggled swiftly to him: 'I'm frightened, Pez—it's getting me—I'm frightened.'

A blast grenade landed in front of them and crushed them between the earth and sky.

Janos almost started up. Pez slammed an arm across his shoulders and pinned him back to the earth. 'Keep still, boy,' he pleaded. 'For Christ sake, keep still. We can't move. We've got to wait till morning. We're in a fold here—we're safe if we keep still.'

Janos' breath was shuddering and his body trembled violently under Pez's arm. 'It's got me, Pez,' he whispered. 'I'm frightened.'

And so, through the long nightmare of darkness, Pez held him to the earth—whispering, pleading with him, and holding his trembling body to the earth.

We are saved.

'B' Company attacks with the first light and springs us from the trap. We are haggard and grimed and grey—our eyes burn red in gaunt faces—our hands tremble.

Pez has to lift Janos to his feet.

'I'm through, boy,' he whispers. 'Never again—I can never go again.'

*

But we didn't have to go again.

Word came through that we were to stay put—patrol our front, but keep out of trouble.

We built our doover tents on the ridge and on the lip of the gully. We corded the muddy track with scrub timber. The Sally tent moved up to us on the ridge and there was the Sally bloke dishing out hot coffee and biscuits.

Strange how you grow accustomed to a piece of earth and it is home. This hostile ridge we stormed foam-flanked became familiar in a day—our land—won with blood. Behind that hummock there, the old soldier, Whispering John, had died; the fixed little grin had snarled back when we found him, showing his stained yellow teeth. Near that pit there, young Regan fell with a bullet in his spine—they say he may never walk again.

We wait.

There is a swift wing unbeating in the sky; there is a high wind that never stirs a leaf, blowing without a ripple over the Pacific and the whole world—a waiting wind. There is a strange and soundless bugle call frozen like a curlew's call midway between the earth and stars.

And at night we lie in our doovers and young Snowy Miller from Don Company up the hill sings the songs—the old songs. He has a choir-boy voice, untrained but sweet and true, and the old songs float down the hill, drifting through the trees…'I Dream of Jeanie' and 'Waken for Me'…

'She's over,' the sig wires said. 'I tell you she's all wrapped up—she's buggerup finish—she's ridge!'

But nobody really believed it.

Then Bairdie came up the track and called us together and read it out to us. A personal letter from the General, almost; assuring us that we had won—innings declared.

And the drums began beating in the hills—they throbbed and boomed through the hills all day and into the night—telling the Kanaka boys with the Nips in the mountains, that it was over—no more hide and seek—time to come home for dinner.

And when the police boys and the carrying parties passed, the boys grinned hugely and stamped their splayed feet in the joyful mud: 'War bin pfinis—bagerup pfinis—Japan man pfinis—hihihihihihi—plenty kai kai, plenty pom pom—war bagerup—pfinis!'

Surely one should dance and sing and pound a comrade on the back—we won! But we feel lost and lonely and there's a breathless wind in the high air. We sit about in our doovers and speak quietly and casually—and it's only when you look at a man's eyes that you realise he is seeing something beyond the mountains and the trees—a vast, slow, broken wheel is turning in the sky—and in some strange way he is unbelieving and afraid of what he sees.

Pez chopped the side out of a biscuit tin and found some black paint somewhere. THE ROAD BACK, he daubed in bold letters and planted it beside their doover, with an arrow pointing back down the track to the sea.

He spent a deal of time outlining to Janos an ambitiously alcoholic project for the first civilised pub they encountered.

It was almost dark on the night of the day the war ended when Janos rose to take the first trick at guard.

'How are you feeling, mate?' asked Pez. 'I'll take it if you like.'

'No, I'm all right.'

'You sure?'

'Yeah,' said Janos with a grin. 'I'm a big boy again now—I'm not afraid of the dark any more.'

He went down to Harry Drew's doover to get the Owen for guard.

Those of us further down the hill heard the single, flat explosion of the shot from the crest of the ridge, and the long cry—stretcher bearers! stretcher bearers!—came pelting down the hill.

We heard their shod feet thudding on the corded track as they ran up the hill and, after a while, we heard them returning—the careful, dragging trample of their feet, as though they carried something heavy.

'What happened?' someone called from the darkness beside the track.

'Owen went off accidentally.'

'Anyone hurt?'

'Yes, Janos.'

'Is he bad?'

'He's dead.'

And the earth stood open to receive its dead.

This man born of woman, who had but a little time of life, lay shrouded in a grey blanket. To lie in cold corruption in the black earth—in the alien earth where the leaves weep for ever for the rainforest.

Pez and Harry Drew and Sunny dug his grave—narrow and not too deep—and the cross is painted that says, NX13686 Private W. E. Janner.

The rest of the platoon, loaded ready for the track, stand bareheaded in the rain. Connell, who came up that morning and had waited for the burial, stands behind Pez.

And when it is done, except for the earth heavy on him, Pez steps forward, and scraping a handful of sticky clay, casts it on him. And Connell steps forward and throws a handful of earth into the pit himself—then walks hurriedly away back down the track.

The platoon moves off and Pez and Harry Drew and Sunny shovel the thick earth furiously and silently into the pit, smooth the mound and plant the cross at the head.

They climb into their packs and Pez picks up the ROAD BACK sign that had stood outside their doover.

He walks to the grave and, bending over awkwardly under the weight of his pack, plants it firmly at the foot, with the arrow pointing away down the track towards the sea.

Harry Drew leads off the track, with Sunny after him.

Pez follows.

The drums are beating in the hills.

Pez sat in his tent at the new camp on the beach, writing a letter.

*Dear Mrs Janner,*

*I am writing this on behalf of the platoon.*

*Your son died saving some of our lives.*

*We were cut off and surrounded and there was a break made through our lines. Bill stopped that breakthrough and saved us. But he was killed doing it.*

*We will never be able to tell you how we felt about him. All we can say is that he died most bravely and he was our friend...*

What the hell! He *could* have died like that a thousand times—instead of the monstrously stupid chance of a gun going off accidentally.

Private W. E. Janner...used to know a man once of that name...Janos we called him—the God that looks forward and back.

Why shouldn't he write a lie like that to her—it could have been the truth. What the hell would she care, anyway? She never really knew him. All she'd want to do would be to cry over him a little.

Not that *we* weep...*our* hearts are dry—but our brother Janos is dead.

Pez walked out of the tent and, in the rich moonlight, ploughed across the unfamiliar sand of the new camp to the beach.

There was a wind blowing high that did not blow. A broken wheel was turning in the sky. There was a bugle call transfixed by the spear of stars, pinned like a curlew call between the earth and sky.

The bay was empty and the seas stretched barren far away. But soon the seas would bring ships and there would be a coming home and a heart singing. We must go on down a long, long track. But at least when he got home there was a door to knock on—even if an uncertain door.

God, there must be a meaning. Fiercely he was certain that there must be a meaning.

Surely, while we live we are not lost.

Oh Janos, Janos my brother!

Surely we are not lost—while we live.

# *Text Classics*

**Dancing on Coral**
**Glenda Adams**
Introduced by Susan Wyndham

**The Commandant**
**Jessica Anderson**
Introduced by Carmen Callil

**Homesickness**
**Murray Bail**
Introduced by Peter Conrad

**Sydney Bridge Upside Down**
**David Ballantyne**
Introduced by Kate De Goldi

**Bush Studies**
**Barbara Baynton**
Introduced by Helen Garner

**The Cardboard Crown**
**Martin Boyd**
Introduced by Brenda Niall

**A Difficult Young Man**
**Martin Boyd**
Introduced by Sonya Hartnett

**Outbreak of Love**
**Martin Boyd**
Introduced by Chris Womersley

**The Australian Ugliness**
**Robin Boyd**
Introduced by Christos Tsiolkas

**All the Green Year**
**Don Charlwood**
Introduced by Michael McGirr

**They Found a Cave**
**Nan Chauncy**
Introduced by John Marsden

**The Even More Complete Book of Australian Verse**
**John Clarke**

**Diary of a Bad Year**
**J. M. Coetzee**
Introduced by Peter Goldsworthy

**Wake in Fright**
**Kenneth Cook**
Introduced by Peter Temple

**The Dying Trade**
**Peter Corris**
Introduced by Charles Waterstreet

**They're a Weird Mob**
**Nino Culotta**
Introduced by Jacinta Tynan

**The Songs of a Sentimental Bloke**
**C. J. Dennis**
Introduced by Jack Thompson

**Careful, He Might Hear You**
**Sumner Locke Elliott**
Introduced by Robyn Nevin

**Fairyland**
**Sumner Locke Elliott**
Introduced by Dennis Altman

**The Explorers**
Edited and introduced by
**Tim Flannery**

**Terra Australis**
**Matthew Flinders**
Introduced by Tim Flannery

**My Brilliant Career**
**Miles Franklin**
Introduced by Jennifer Byrne

**Such is Life**
**Joseph Furphy**
Introduced by David Malouf

**The Fringe Dwellers**
**Nene Gare**
Introduced by Melissa Lucashenko

**Cosmo Cosmolino**
**Helen Garner**
Introduced by Ramona Koval

**Wish**
**Peter Goldsworthy**
Introduced by James Bradley

**Dark Places**
**Kate Grenville**
Introduced by Louise Adler

**The Quiet Earth**
**Craig Harrison**
Introduced by Bernard Beckett

**Down in the City**
**Elizabeth Harrower**
Introduced by Delia Falconer

**The Long Prospect**
**Elizabeth Harrower**
Introduced by Fiona McGregor

**The Watch Tower**
**Elizabeth Harrower**
Introduced by Joan London

**The Long Green Shore**
**John Hepworth**
Introduced by Lloyd Jones

**The Mystery of a Hansom Cab**
**Fergus Hume**
Introduced by Simon Caterson

**The Unknown Industrial Prisoner**
**David Ireland**
Introduced by Peter Pierce

**The Glass Canoe**
**David Ireland**
Introduced by Nicolas Rothwell

**A Woman of the Future**
**David Ireland**
Introduced by Kate Jennings

**Eat Me**
**Linda Jaivin**
Introduced by Krissy Kneen

**Julia Paradise**
**Rod Jones**
Introduced by Emily Maguire

**The Jerilderie Letter**
**Ned Kelly**
Introduced by Alex McDermott

**Bring Larks and Heroes**
**Thomas Keneally**
Introduced by Geordie Williamson

**Strine**
**Afferbeck Lauder**
Introduced by John Clarke

**The Young Desire It**
**Kenneth Mackenzie**
Introduced by David Malouf

**Stiff**
**Shane Maloney**
Introduced by Lindsay Tanner

**The Middle Parts of Fortune**
**Frederic Manning**
Introduced by Simon Caterson

**Selected Stories**
**Katherine Mansfield**
Introduced by Emily Perkins

**The Home Girls**
**Olga Masters**
Introduced by Geordie Williamson

**Amy's Children**
**Olga Masters**
Introduced by Eva Hornung

**The Scarecrow**
**Ronald Hugh Morrieson**
Introduced by Craig Sherborne

**The Dig Tree**
**Sarah Murgatroyd**
Introduced by Geoffrey Blainey

**A Lifetime on Clouds**
**Gerald Murnane**
Introduced by Andy Griffiths

**The Plains**
**Gerald Murnane**
Introduced by Wayne Macauley

**The Odd Angry Shot**
**William Nagle**
Introduced by Paul Ham

**Life and Adventures 1776–1801**
**John Nicol**
Introduced by Tim Flannery

**Death in Brunswick**
**Boyd Oxlade**
Introduced by Shane Maloney

**Swords and Crowns and Rings**
**Ruth Park**
Introduced by Alice Pung

**The Watcher in the Garden**
**Joan Phipson**
Introduced by Margo Lanagan

**Maurice Guest**
**Henry Handel Richardson**
Introduced by Carmen Callil

**The Getting of Wisdom**
**Henry Handel Richardson**
Introduced by Germaine Greer

**The Fortunes of Richard Mahony**
**Henry Handel Richardson**
Introduced by Peter Craven

**Rose Boys**
**Peter Rose**
Introduced by Brian Matthews

**Hills End**
**Ivan Southall**
Introduced by James Moloney

**Ash Road**
**Ivan Southall**
Introduced by Maurice Saxby

**Lillipilly Hill**
**Eleanor Spence**
Introduced by Ursula Dubosarsky

**The Women in Black**
**Madeleine St John**
Introduced by Bruce Beresford

**The Essence of the Thing**
**Madeleine St John**
Introduced by Helen Trinca

**Jonah**
**Louis Stone**
Introduced by Frank Moorhouse

**An Iron Rose**
**Peter Temple**
Introduced by Les Carlyon

**1788**
**Watkin Tench**
Introduced by Tim Flannery

**The House that Was Eureka**
**Nadia Wheatley**
Introduced by Toni Jordan

**Happy Valley**
**Patrick White**
Introduced by Peter Craven

**I for Isobel**
**Amy Witting**
Introduced by Charlotte Wood

**I Own the Racecourse!**
**Patricia Wrightson**
Introduced by Kate Constable

**textclassics.com.au**